MURDER
MOST
FOWL

THE FREE RANGE DETECTIVE AGENCY

JED LYNCH

Murder Most Fowl

First published in 2019 by
Little Island Books
7 Kenilworth Park
Dublin 6W
Ireland

Print ISBN: 978-1-912417-41-4
Ebook (Kindle) ISBN: 978-1-912417-55-1
Ebook (other platforms) ISBN: 978-1-912417-54-4

A British Library Cataloguing in Publication record for this book is available from the British Library.

Illustrated by Stephen Stone
Designed by Catherine Gaffney
Copy-edited by Emma Dunne
Printed in Poland by L&C Printing

Little Island has received funding to support this book from the Arts Council of Ireland.

10 9 8 7 6 5 4 3 2 1

For

DARRACH

and

CILLIAN

1

THE DOORBELL

I was just tucking into my morning bowl of Shredded Worms when the doorbell rang.

OK, so first of all I suppose I should explain about the Shredded Worms. My name is Seamus the Turkey, and I'm a shamus. A shamus is just another word for a private detective. And a turkey is just another word for a big chicken-shaped bird that's terrible at flying and terrified of Christmas. Like it says on my business cards:

The Free Range Detective Agency is a big name for a very small operation: me (the private detective) and Auntie Et (my fearsome secretary). Unfortunately for me, I don't seem to be a very good private detective. Or at least not a very popular one. On this particular morning I hadn't had a case to solve since the Case of the Rampaging Rhinoceros three months before. To save money, I had recently started eating nothing but four bowls of Shredded Worms a day. In spite of this, my money was nearly gone. If I didn't get another case soon, I was going to run out of Shredded Worms and have to start eating my business cards.

After I picked my spoon back out of my Shredded Worms, and my lower jaw off the floor, I started to pull myself together. My first thought was that I must be imagining the doorbell ringing. Maybe it was a hallucination brought on by all the Shredded Worms. After all, the box said they should be eaten as part of a healthy and balanced diet, and my diet was neither. I stole a glance over at Auntie Et to see if she had heard the doorbell as well.

I'm not sure how Auntie Et got her name. I presume her parents didn't look at her when she was born and think, 'Wow, this baby looks just like someone's aunt! Let's call her Auntie!' And she's certainly not my aunt – she's a hyena. She is also probably the scariest person I've ever met. Most hyenas have a very creepy and weird laugh. But what's even creepier and weirder than a hyena's creepy and weird laugh is a hyena who never, ever laughs. Auntie Et is one of those. In all the time she's been with me, I've never seen her crack even the first hint of a smile. It's deeply unsettling.

I'm not entirely sure what she does all day – there are hardly ever any calls to take or letters to file away –

but then I'm not entirely sure what I pay her. She's in charge of the accounts, and I'm afraid to ask. Though it can't be very much, given how few cases I've had. I'd say that she's happy to work for next to nothing, but then I'm not sure she's ever been happy with anything in her life.

She met my glance with a fierce glare. 'I suppose you'll want me to answer that, then? Hmmm?'

As usual with Auntie Et, I felt like I was imposing on her just by looking in her direction. 'Um, well, if you wouldn't mind? Just hold them for a minute or two while I get myself ready.'

Getting myself ready involved hiding as many of the dirty bowls, cups and plates as I could lay my wings on, before shoving the sleeping bag behind my desk and stuffing the pillows into a spare cupboard. I had been sleeping in my office for a couple of weeks, ever since my ex-landlord had kicked me out of my apartment for not paying the rent. Any of the rent. Ever. I have to say, I'd have kicked me out too if I was him. Although I'd like to think that I wouldn't have kicked me quite so many times while I was kicking me out. My tail-feathers were so bruised from all of the kicking that it was still sore to sit down two weeks later.

Unfortunately, while I could do something to improve the look of the office-cum-sleeping-quarters, there was very little I could do to improve the look of myself. Between eating nothing but Shredded Worms, worrying about where my next case was going to come from and sleeping on the very prickly and far-too-small office couch, I wasn't looking my best. Hoping that I

sounded more confident and less bedraggled than I felt,
I called out to Auntie Et.

'Please show them in, Auntie.'

2

A FELINE VISITOR

'So this is what a private detective looks like.' She was a very rich-looking cat with a cruel-looking smile. Her voice was a low purr, velvety and slightly playful. I felt like I was a mouse that she had caught and she was deciding if she should kill me or let me go. Either way, she was definitely planning on having some fun before she was done with me.

I had a bad feeling about this.

'Only when he thinks no-one will be calling around.' It was pretty bad as replies go, but I was tired and nervous and acutely aware of Auntie Et glaring over from her desk in the corner. She had introduced the cat as Ms Ermine, then taken up her position, pen in paw, to record the important details of the meeting. She was looking even more ill-tempered than usual – she had clearly taken an immediate and intense dislike to Ms Ermine. I could understand why. Ms Ermine had the air of someone who was used to people doing what she very sweetly asked them to because of her good looks and dazzling smile. And her perfectly manicured and razor-sharp claws looked like they could be used to help out when asking wasn't enough.

She smiled, showing a row of pointed pearly teeth. She was enjoying making me uncomfortable. 'Looks like you haven't had anyone call around in quite a while, Mr Seamus,' she said, her eyes lazily taking in the office.

While I had managed to hide most of the dirty bowls, cups and plates, I wasn't able to hide the unmistakably grubby and neglected look of the place.

Auntie Et gave one of her warning coughs. Clearly, she was unimpressed by all of this small talk. It was time to get down to business.

'It's just Seamus, no mister. And how can I help you, Ms Ermine?'

'It's *Miss* Ermine, I'm afraid. And like you, Seamus, I have no mister. Although I used to.' She touched a fancy gold locket that hung on a chain around her neck and gave a cold little smile. 'Poor Mr Ermine, he worked himself into the ground.'

'He died of exhaustion? Overwork?'

'Oh no, he was an engineer working on a tunnel that mysteriously collapsed. Buried alive. *Terrible* way to go.'

The words she said were sad, but she smiled a bitter, cruel smile as she said them, and a little voice inside my head told me to be very, very careful with the tragically widowed Miss Ermine. In case the little voice inside my head wasn't enough, Auntie Et gave a particularly sharp cough-and-scowl combination. Her message was clear: be very, very, *very* careful of this cat.

On the other hand, Miss Ermine looked pretty swish with her fur coat and her fancy gold jewellery, and I didn't fancy eating only Shredded Worms for the rest of my life. If I played my cards right, I felt I might be able to rent a bedroom with an actual bed in it. Or at least get a blow-up mattress for the office. Thinking of all the nights of fantastic sleep that lay ahead of me, I decided to proceed, but with caution. I leaned back in my chair and put on my best tell-me-all-about-it voice.

'Well, Miss Ermine, why don't you take a seat and fill me in on this problem of yours?'

Miss Ermine took a flask from under her fur coat, daintily picked up a cup and poured herself a drink. I wasn't sure what the drink was – maybe it was milk, maybe it was juice, maybe it was something made from the tears of all the mice she had ever captured. Whatever it was, I hoped it was strong enough to kill off any mould or small animals that might be in the cup because I was fairly sure I hadn't washed it out in quite a while.

'I'm not sure that I can, Seamus,' she began.

'Oh? You're afraid that someone will find out that you spilled the beans? Let the cat out of the bag, as it were? I'm completely discreet, Miss Ermine, I assure you. My clients' secrets are my secrets.'

'Oh no, it's not that. It's just that I'm not sure there *is* a problem. Not yet, anyway.'

This was just plain odd. Who goes to a private detective when they *don't* have a problem? It's like going to a hospital to tell them that you've never felt better, and would the nice doctor mind examining you, please?

Auntie Et must have felt the same way – she had had enough of the fur-coat-wearing cat. 'Miss Ermine, while Mr Seamus is too polite to say so, he is tremendously busy at present. And while he is an extremely effective private detective, even he would find it difficult to solve a problem that you do not have. To avoid wasting any of our time further, it might be best to end this interview now, hmmm?'

Miss Ermine's smile tightened further as she pointedly turned her back to Auntie. 'Well, Seamus, I thought that you were the boss here, but if you're not, I suppose I can just leave right now ...'

She trailed off, her eyes hooked on me. I reckoned it might be worth humouring Miss Ermine a little more. That fur coat did look very expensive.

'Let's not be too hasty to judge, Auntie. Just because Miss Ermine doesn't have a problem right now doesn't mean she won't have one in the future. And maybe we could help stop that problem from becoming a problem at all.'

Miss Ermine relaxed a little, and her smile broadened as she purred. 'I knew you would understand, Seamus.' On the other hand, Auntie Et looked like she had suddenly started chomping on a mouthful of broken glass. I expected steam to start coming out from her nose at any point. That crack about me being the boss had clearly stung her.

To make sure that Auntie Et saw where I was coming from, I decided to stress the money angle. 'I am afraid, Miss Ermine, that this kind of non-problem case can be extremely tricky. Extraodinarily tricky. Extraordinar-emely tricky, if you will. You start off thinking that you have no problem at all but, before you know it, there are problems popping up everywhere. And, unfortunately, that means money. Now, it's my policy never to fleece my customers — unless they're sheep, of course, and they're in need of a good fleecing, in which case I use the not-too-rusty shears I keep in the bottom drawer of my office desk. They're actually garden shears instead of sheep-shearing shears, but I find that they do the job just as well.'

Miss Ermine looked a little confused, and I realised that I may have strayed slightly off topic.

'Anyway, enough about sheep. Let's get back to the money, Miss Ermine. I will need a starting fee of €500 and a daily retainer of €100.'

Miss Ermine spread her paws. 'That won't be a problem, I assure you. For the service you'll be providing, I'm sure I'll be getting *wonderful* value.'

Again she smiled, showing her exceptionally white, sparkly and, above all, sharp teeth. And the little voice inside my bird-brained head started up again, saying there was something not quite right about all of this — a voice that I really should have listened to because if I had I'd have saved myself a whole bucket-load of trouble. But a much bigger voice inside my head kept jumping up and down, shouting: '€100 a day! €100 a day! €100 a day!'

The little voice never had a chance.

'In fact,' she continued, 'why don't I just give you a week's pay in advance, to show you how much faith I have in you?'

She pulled out a wad of €100 notes and peeled off twelve of them. My wings trembled as I took the money – I'd never seen this much cash outside of a bank before – but I tried to play it cool as I slid the notes into the top drawer of the desk.

Auntie Et scowled at me. It was clear that she didn't want me to take on this case, no matter how many €100 notes were involved, but she had decided to keep her coughs to herself for now.

'All right then, Miss Ermine,' I said, trying to keep my excitement under control, 'tell me about your problem that's not a problem. Yet.'

3

THE CAT'S TALE

'Well, Mr Seamus, I mean, *Seamus*, I work at a club. I'm a singer – what they call the star attraction.' Miss Ermine smirked and I thought that, whatever *they* might call her, *she* would certainly call herself the star attraction. If she were chocolate, she would have eaten herself by now. She continued on, her smirk widening. 'You might have heard of the place – the Blue Chameleon?'

Well, that would explain all the €100 notes. The Blue Chameleon was the swankiest club in town – even a turkey like me had to have heard of it. A fruit juice there would set you back a week's pay, and that was presuming someone had actually paid you that week. I usually wouldn't be able to afford a single sheet of toilet roll there, not to mind an actual drink.

'Not only have I heard of it,' I said recklessly, 'I've been there, uh, loads of times.' I'd never been within twenty feet of the door of the place, and would probably be plucked, trussed and roasted for dinner if I tried to get inside, but I felt I had to seem like I knew what I was doing to justify all of those €100 notes.

'How silly of me, of course you have,' Miss Ermine trilled, as she flashed a wolfish grin, 'though I wonder why I didn't recognise you. Or, for that matter, why you didn't recognise *me*.'

'Well, ehm, it's always just so dark in there,' I stammered. 'You'd think they'd be able to afford a few more lightbulbs, when it costs that much to get in. And, you know, us turkeys wouldn't be known for our night vision. There's a reason those things in the road are called cat's eyes and not turkey's eyes, after all. If they were turkey's eyes, there'd probably be loads of crashes all the time. Well, all the time at night anyway.'

Miss Ermine's grin widened even further. 'Of course, of course,' she murmured soothingly, 'my mistake. If I may continue?'

'Oh, please do.' I attempted to re-gather what was left of my composure, which at that point seemed to be scattered all around the office.

While I was distracted, Auntie Et attempted to move things along. 'As quickly as possible, Miss Ermine. We don't want this to take longer than it needs to, hmmm?'

While pointedly ignoring Auntie Et's contribution, the cat took up her story again. 'There's a rival club – the Clubfooted Pigeon – that has been trying to take business from us over the last few years. Every week or so they send a few thugs over to the Blue Chameleon to cause a scene and try to get us shut down or scare off our customers. And the problem, Seamus, is that there hasn't been a problem for weeks. They haven't sent anyone over to rough up our customers or to start fights with the staff. I don't know what it means, but I'm afraid that they're planning something big. And I'd like *you* to find out what it is.'

She turned on her biggest Bambi eyes as she looked right at me, but I was a private detective who had gone to private detecting school and everything, and I wasn't about to stop privately detecting just because some cat fluttered her eyelashes at me.

'Well, Miss Ermine, why doesn't your boss hire someone to look into it? That would seem the sensible thing to do. After all, you're just a singer at the club. No offence meant.'

'None taken, I'm sure.' Her voice was still soft, but with a harder edge – she evidently didn't like being described as 'just' a singer. I thought I heard a strange sound coming from Auntie Et, which might have been the sound of her facial muscles resisting as she attempted to smile, but I couldn't look to find out. I needed to keep focused on my client, who continued, 'I don't want to worry poor Mr Masher, in case it's nothing.'

For the second time this morning, I had to pick my lower jaw off the floor. 'Mr Masher? Mr Maurice Masher? He's the owner of the Blue Chameleon?'

'Of course. Why is that so shocking to you?'

Where to begin? As I said, the Blue Chameleon was the swankiest club in town, where the super-rich went to hang out. And now it turned out that it was owned by Mr Maurice Masher, a big brawny boar who also happened to be my low-down turkey-kicking ex-landlord. For some reason, though, I decided not to share this titbit of information just yet. Best keep my relationship to Mr Masher under wraps for the time being.

'No particular reason – I must be confusing him with someone else.' The cat didn't look convinced, so I decided that attack was the best form of defence. 'So, why do you care so much about the Blue Chameleon to go out of your way like this? It could end up costing you a small fortune, after all.' After all, I certainly hoped that it would.

'When my husband died, I needed something to give my life meaning, something to get out of bed for. The Blue Chameleon became that something, so I care about it very much. And my husband left me a middling-sized fortune when he died, so I'm not worried about spending a small one on this.'

She stood up. The tone of the meeting had become a lot frostier, and I presumed that she was looking to put an end to it.

'I trust I can count on your discretion in this matter, Seamus? It would do untold damage if word were to get out that the Blue Chameleon was worried about anything the Clubfooted Pigeon might be getting up to.'

'Of course, I understand just how delicate the matter is.'

She stopped with one paw on the door handle, her well-manicured claws extended. 'And one more thing. If you do find some way to *permanently* deal with the nuisance that is the Clubfooted Pigeon, there'll be a €1,000 bonus in it for you.'

I nearly fell off my chair with excitement. That dead husband of hers must have been loaded – with that bonus I could probably rent an apartment with two bedrooms and sleep in a different one each night. 'I'll see what I can do,' I said, playing it cool. 'And if I need to get in touch with you?'

'I would have thought that should be *no* problem for an eminent sleuth like yourself.' That chilly mocking smile again. 'Find me at the club. You know the one – after all, you've been there *loads* of times. Just ask for Imelda. Imelda Ermine.'

And with that she turned the handle, opened the door and was gone.

4

BREAKING WIND AND ENTERING

The Clubfooted Pigeon was the biggest club on the baddest side of town. Its clientele were the less posh local criminals, the ones who wouldn't say 'Excuse me' before they robbed your wallet or knifed you in the ribs. It prided itself on its tough-guy image and seemed to hire its bouncers for the size of their muscles rather than, for instance, their ability to talk in complete sentences. The bouncers were huge tattoo-covered pigs. They had piercings through their ears, lips, noses – you name it, they probably had it pierced. One even had his knuckles pierced, which seemed excessive to me. They spent most of their time flexing their muscles and farting loudly. I wondered if the two were connected. I could only imagine what they'd smell like up close.

I wouldn't have to imagine for long. I'd decided this would be the best place to get to work on my new case, so once I got my nerves under control I was going to head in there and experience that piggy smell up close and personal. My plan was to get in and interview the owner to figure out the lay of the land, and then get out again before I picked up some kind of mad smelly pig disease.

I was feeling a lot better that morning than I'd felt in ages. The previous evening I had given Auntie Et a €100 on-the-spot bonus and then gone out and had my first non-Shredded Worms meal in a fortnight. It had been so long since I'd eaten proper food that I had forgotten how good grub burgers and chicken nuggets could taste. (The nuggets weren't really made from chickens because a turkey eating a chicken would be fairly gross. They were just chicken-flavoured. Which I suppose is still a little bit gross, but a big bit delicious.) Then I had bought a camp bed for the office, so I'd slept like a log – a log with feathers and a beak and Fireman Freddo pyjamas on, but a log all the same.

In this happy-go-lucky mood even the muscle-bound bouncers couldn't make me nervous for long. I reckoned I should just grab the pig by the horns, as it were, and get it over with. So I marched up to them, refusing to let the smell ruin my sunny disposition.

'How're we getting on, lads? Did ye have a late night last night? Seems like ye skipped the bath this morning.'

'Whut you wunt?' growled one of the bouncers. Never mind roast beef, I thought to myself, this little piggy took steroids and did loads of press-ups.

'I just need to have a quick chat with the owner, lads, if ye wouldn't mind.'

'Yer whut?' This time it was the one with the pierced knuckles who spoke. Or grunted. Or maybe sprunted.

He was clearly confused by my approach. Maybe it was the use of the word 'wouldn't'. Or possibly the use of the word 'the'.

'No way, he nut here,' snarled the other. He was clearly

the brains of the operation. Or the brain of the operation. 'Brains' plural was probably a bit generous.

I had thought that this might happen and had my cover story ready. Bouncers really don't like private detectives – after all, we might start enquiring what exactly they had done to Benny the Bunny to stop him entering the club the previous week, and why Benny could only hop in circles now and cried every time he saw a carrot. So, as I said, I had my cover story ready.

'Well, that's a shame, because he has won the top prize in our weekly jumbo raffle! But if he's not here now to accept the prize then it'll go to someone else. So are you *sure* he isn't around?'

Their brows furrowed, their eyes widened and I thought I could hear their brains creaking under the strain of all this new information.

'How we know you nut tellin lies?' asked the smarter of the two after a veeerrry looonnnggg pause. At this stage the other bouncer had given up trying to follow what was going on. The word 'accept' had probably been the final straw for him. Now he was scratching himself and practising making angry faces. Or maybe he always looked like that.

'Well, of course, gentlemen – I have his winning ticket here with me.' I took a crumpled raffle ticket I had bought the previous Christmas out of my coat pocket and waved it under their noses. 'And I also have this official letter to tell him how to collect his winnings.' With a flourish, I produced from my other pocket a very official-looking letter from my ex-landlord Maurice Masher telling me I had two days to pay the rent I owed or I'd find myself out on my ear. As it turned out, I didn't pay the rent I owed and instead of my ear I ended up out on my very bruised tail-feathers.

The smarter of the piggy pair grabbed the letter from me and peered at it. Then he turned it the right way up and peered at it again. It didn't make any difference – we all know that pigs can't read. He sniffed the letter as if that might give him some clue as to its contents.

After another very long pause, he grunted. 'I bring dis to de boss.'

'Eh, no, no, that won't work, sorry.' Him bringing my ex-landlord's letter to his boss wasn't part of the plan. Even though he couldn't read, his boss would definitely be able to, so I'd never get to see the head honcho if Ein-swine here trundled off with my eviction notice. 'According to the rules of the raffle, I have to deliver the official letter myself, by hand, as an official representative. Otherwise it's not officially official. Officially.'

Another pause, while the pig's grey matter went into overdrive. After what seemed like an age, he came to a decision. 'OK. I bring you. We go now.'

He turned to his partner with the pierced knuckles, who was still scratching away at himself. 'He come wit me. I buck soon. You stay. You in churge.' And before waiting for his colleague to understand what had been said – we didn't want to be waiting all day, after all – we went in through the door.

As I stepped inside and the door closed behind me, the first thing that hit me was the dark. The second thing that hit me was a small table of some kind, which I nearly fell over because of the aforementioned dark. And the third thing that hit me was the smell, which nearly made me fall over again because of its sheer awfulness. The place smelled of stale food and sweat and farting bouncers, and even worse things that I didn't want to think about. In spite of the increased danger of falling flat on my beak, maybe the dark was a good thing. It meant that I couldn't see what was causing all of the smells. It was still only the middle of the morning, so the club was eerily quiet. I had no doubt that by evening it'd be a whole lot louder, and probably even smellier.

My guide seemed to know his way without looking, and I had to hurry to keep up with his snorting and grunting. Down a long corridor, through some curtains, around a corner, down metal stairs, more curtains, and we were standing outside a plain black door. He raised a large fist to bang on it, and I quickly put up a wing to stop him.

'The official letter, I need to give it to him myself – remember? In order for everything to be officially official.' Another by-now-familiar pause, then he handed over the letter with a grunt.

'And one more thing,' I said hurriedly, interrupting his knock for a second time. 'I need to tell him myself, in private.' It wouldn't look great if the pig were to tell his boss that I had a jumbo prize for him, when I had nothing more than a crumpled raffle ticket and an angry letter.

Again he paused, then nodded his agreement. 'OK. Now I knuck. Dat OK wit you?'

'Sure. Knock yourself out.' I half-hoped he would. His muscles were making me nervous. If anything went wrong and his boss decided to have him kick me out of the office, I felt there was a good chance that I'd land all the way over on the other side of town.

Without knocking himself out, the bouncer gave three booming knocks on the door.

5

SSSIMON SSSAYSSS

I'd heard that the head of the Clubfooted Pigeon was extremely secretive and that he was rarely seen in public. I'd heard that the club was named after his favourite food: pigeon. I'd heard that he was an extremely devious and sneaky character. And I'd heard that he trusted absolutely no-one, to the extent that he didn't have a right-hand man. Or a left-hand man. But I suppose that kind of made sense because he didn't have a right hand. Or a left hand. He was called Simon, and he wasn't just sneaky. He was snakey.

Simon was a snake. And not just any snake. He was a deadly black mamba. And right now he was looking directly at me.

'Ssso, you have sssomething for me?'

The pig had entered, announced that I had something for his boss and left. Feeling like a fool for having asked him to leave, I now desperately wished that he'd stayed. Whatever else he'd do to me, the bouncer probably wouldn't eat me. Unfortunately, the same couldn't be said for his boss. Or, should I say, for hisss bosss.

'Well, ehm, not exactly.' I had broken out in a cold sweat and was pretty sure all of my feathers were trembling. If I wasn't careful I'd soon start clucking and running around in circles out of sheer nervousness.

'Not exsssactly? Missster Turkey, thisss isss a very sssimple matter. Either you have sssomething for me or you do not. There isss no other opssshion.'

'Well, in a manner of speaking, I suppose I have, then.'

'In what *particular* manner of ssspeaking would that be, Missster Turkey?'

I'd heard that snakes didn't really smell but they tasted the air with their tongues instead. His tongue was darting in and out of his mouth now, and I had no doubt that he could taste my fear. And that he was enjoying it.

'I think there might have been a misunderstanding. Your bouncers might have got the wrong end of the stick.'

'If you like, Missster Turkey, I can have Sssnot come back in here and sssshow you what the wrong end of the ssstick *really* looksss like. And then he'll quite happily ssskewer you with it.'

The snake smiled, showing his enormous fangs. It was a wonder he didn't cut himself, they looked so sharp. Animals with pointy teeth had begun to feature far too prominently in my life, as far as I was concerned. Still, I had to ask – what did he mean by 'snot'? Hoping that he wouldn't notice the quick change of subject, I said, 'What do you mean by "snot"?'

The smiled widened. 'Not "what", Missster Turkey, but "who". Sssnot isss the fine sssspessimen of a pig who brought you in here. No doubt you alssso met his asssosssiate, Booger, outssside. I can have them come back *inssside* if you like. Then maybe we could sssee what *your* insssidesss look like, maybe?'

'I really don't think that will be necessary.'

The snake reared up. He had obviously realised that I had lied to get into his office, and he no longer seemed amused about it. '*I* will desside what isss and isss not nesssesssary, Missster Turkey, not you. Asss I'm sssshure you are aware, my name isss Missster Sssimon. Asss in "Sssimon Sssaysss". And now Sssimon sssaysss, ssstart talking before I losssse my patienssse. It hasss almosssst run out.'

I felt like running out after it, but figured I wouldn't make it out of the club in one piece if I did. I'd be lucky to make it out in fewer than four pieces.

'Well, Mr Simon, sir, I just have a few questions for you.' Maybe it was his slightly hypnotic eyes, maybe it was the panic I felt rising up inside me, but I decided I had better come clean. 'I'm a private detective, you see, and I'm on a case.'

Mr Simon, it turned out, did not like private detectives. Not even a teensy-weensy bit. This didn't exactly come as a surprise, but it did make my situation that bit more perilous.

'What?! You come in here, to my offissse, under falssse pretensssesss, and you're nothing more than a ssshamusss?'

'Actually, I'm Seamus the Shamus. Funny coincidence, isn't it? I have business cards and everything. Well, I did have business cards until I ate them by mistake last week. I thought they were Limited Edition Shredded Worm Crackers.' I was babbling now, talking rubbish while I tried to think of something to get me out of the office alive.

'Missster Turkey-Ssshamusss, I think I have heard quite enough. Sssimon sssaysss that the penalty for wasssting my time thisss morning ... isss *death*. Sssnot will be happy to help you leave thisss offissse. And thisss world.'

With a flick of his tail, the snake pulled a cord behind his desk. I knew that I only had a few seconds before my goose was cooked.

For once, a good idea popped into my head at just the right time.

'I wouldn't do that if I were you, Simon. You see, I've been in touch with the police. I told them I was coming down here, and that if I didn't call back to the station this afternoon then they should open a murder enquiry. With you as the main suspect.' Of course, none of this was true, but if I could convince the snake that it was I might be able to save myself from a sudden and very unhappy ending.

Simon sat back and considered me coldly. I could see that he didn't believe me, but he wasn't a hundred per cent sure that I was bluffing. The question was, was he sure enough to risk a murder investigation? The last thing he wanted to do was give the police an excuse to snoop around his club.

'That isss very clever, Missster Turkey-Ssshamusss. In fact, I think it isss *too* clever. I don't believe that you did call to the polissse thisss morning. I don't think that they are exsssspecting you thisss afternoon. And I don't think that there will be any murder invessstigation when you disssappear.'

I could hear heavy footsteps coming down the corridor outside. I needed to hurry.

'OK, Simon. But what if you're wrong? Is it worth risking everything? For one turkey? I don't think jail would suit you. They probably wouldn't have a prison uniform in your size – extra long.'

'I can very easssily check, you know. I could have sssomeone ring the polissse and sssee if they know any Turkey-Ssshamusssesss.'

There were three loud bangs on the door. My buddy Snot was back.

'Of course you can. But if you do that, they'll get suspicious. Why would someone from your club be asking about a Turkey-Shamus? They'd definitely come looking for me then. And when the Turkey-Shamus turns out to be missing, presumed dead, guess who they'll centre their investigation around? I'm sure they're just itching to come down here with a search warrant and have a good poke around. And I'm pretty sure they'd find a lot of things that would interest them.'

The snake frowned. He knew that I had him. There were three more bangs on the door. I reckoned it needed to be reinforced just to withstand Snot's knocks.

'Buss? You OK dere?' Snot's concern was touching.

There was another long pause while Simon stared at me. Then he blinked slowly. 'Perhapsss you are right, Missster Turkey-Ssshamusss. I will let you go. *Thisss* time.'

Another three bangs on the door. 'Buss? Will I bust down de door?'

'No, Sssnot. I think it would be bessst if you jussst turn the handle and open it inssstead.'

Snot entered, somewhat disappointed. 'He butherin you, buss? I take care of him?' Snot cracked his knuckles enthusiastically in anticipation.

'Not thisss time, Sssnot. You can sssimply essscort Missster Turkey off the premisssesss.'

Snot's brow furrowed even more than usual. 'Dat de code wurd for dat I kill him?' Clearly he didn't do discreet and had big problems with subtlety.

'No, Sssnot, not thisss time. Missster Turkey hasss sssome friendsss in the polissse.'

'OK. I take him out and nut kill him.'

'Just a second.' I didn't want to leave Simon's office without something useful for the case, especially after I had nearly got myself made extinct to get in there. I felt that he wouldn't put up with a lot of subtle questioning, so I decided to get right to the point. 'What are you planning for the Blue Chameleon? I have sources that tell me you've something up your sleeve for it. As it were.'

Simon smiled. 'Ssso thisss isss your quessstion? I'm afraid, Missster Turkey-Ssshamusss, that you have been misssinformed. I have absssolutely no planss regarding that club. And if anything ssshould happen to the Blue Chameleon, or itsss charming owner, it would have nothing to do with me. Now, Sssnot, pleassse help Missster Turkey-Ssshamusss leave the premisssesss, with the minimum of fusss and the maximum of ssspeed.'

6

GOING TO
SEE THE DOC

I pondered my next move over a cup of coffee in Enzo's Family-Friendly Fryathon. The coffee was bad but at least it was cheap, and they didn't guilt you into buying a new one every ten minutes. They also served anything you might possibly like to eat, as long as it was fried. Fried eggs, fried bananas, fried Mars bars, fried maggots. Like I said, anything. I ordered a fried beetle sandwich, on fried bread of course. The great thing about fried beetle sandwiches is that the beetles are still good and crunchy when you bite into them. As I munched away on all that fried deliciousness, I turned the case over in my mind.

I had been lucky to get out of the Clubfooted Pigeon alive, but now that I was out of there I didn't think I had learned a whole lot. Sure, the bouncers were a bit dim, but I knew that already. And Simon was definitely keen to avoid having the police come down and take a good look around his club, but that was probably the case with club owners everywhere. On the other hand, he had talked about how it would be a shame if something happened to the owner of the Blue Chameleon. Which was odd because I'd never mentioned the Blue Chameleon's owner, my ex-landlord Maurice Masher – I had only asked Simon about his interest in the club. So maybe he *was* plotting something. Or maybe it was just an innocent remark, even though 'innocent' and Simon the Snake didn't go very well together. The problem was, I had no proof. I didn't even have any new clues to follow up.

I was also beginning to have my suspicions about my old buddy, Maurice the turkey-kicking ex-landlord Masher. Apart from his disturbing love of kicking birds, he seemed to be unnaturally close to Miss Imelda Ermine, which struck me as a very bad sign of his character. There was something dodgy about the whole thing.

Chewing on these issues, as well as chewing on my fried-beetles-in-fried-bread sandwich, I decided it was time to call in to the Blue Chameleon and have a chat with Maurice Masher himself. Partly to be as prepared as possible for this meeting, and partly to put off meeting the turkey-kicking Mr Masher for a little bit longer, I thought it would be a good idea to get some more background info on him. After all, I hadn't known until Imelda Ermine walked into my life that he was the owner of the Blue Chameleon. What other secrets might he be hiding that I should know about?

There was only one person I could turn to at a time like this. I knew him from detecting school. (You thought I'd made up the bit about detecting school, didn't you? Well, I didn't.) These days he kept a very low profile. So low, in fact, that he was usually underground. Which made him perfect for digging up dirt on people. He was (rather unfortunately) called Jebediah Dockleaf, or Doc for short, and he was a mole.

Doc settled back into one of the well-worn armchairs in his subterranean sitting room. He didn't need any encouragement to start dishing the dirt on Maurice Masher. Doc had been my PE teacher at detecting school, and it turned out that Maurice had been Doc's PE teacher years before. Once I got over my initial shock at hearing that Maurice Masher had been a detective himself, I was able to tune back in to what Doc was telling me.

'Think of the nicest person you can,' he began, 'someone who is … caring. Who never laughs at you when you fall over. Who would always be kind and … reassuring. And who would never make fun of your bad posture and … terrible eyesight. Got it?'

I nodded. That actually wasn't a bad description of Doc himself. Doc's PE classes were probably my favourite classes of all when I was in detective school. They were a great opportunity to catch up on my mid-morning napping. Doc was just too gentle and polite to force us to actually do any physical activity.

'Now imagine the person who is the … opposite of that nicest person. That opposite-person, that's … Maurice Masher. He would yell at us in PE class. "Come on! Second is the first loser!" I used to dream of being first in PE class someday, even if it was just the first loser. But it never happened. Once I was in a race on my own, against the clock, and the clock … finished before me. It was faster running out of batteries than … I was running the race.'

Doc paused to catch his breath. He had never been much good at public speaking, what with all his … long pauses in the … middle of his … sentences. And at the start and the end of his sentences as well. I had heard that he wasn't actually that old, but he looked absolutely ancient.

Some people are born old-looking and get younger-looking as they grow up. Doc wasn't one of those. He was probably old-looking when he was born, and he just got even more ancient-looking the older he got.

'Jeez, Doc, he sounds pretty awful. So how come he wasn't teaching by the time I was in detecting school?'

'They took his detecting licence away from him after ... the Case of the Disappearing Dalmatians. No-one ever solved it, but by the time it finished there were ... three dead Dalmatians, a dead heat, a dead battery, and a dead dodo. Although the dodo may have been dead to ... begin with. After that, he was never allowed to practice as a detective again. He became bitter and ... twisted. Or, should I say, he became even *more* ... bitter and twisted.'

'So how come they took his licence away? Was he found guilty in that Disappearing Dalmatians case?'

'Nothing was ever proved, but he was ... the only suspect in the case. It was a work accident that looked far too ... accidental-on-purpose, but no-one was ever able to pin anything on him. Still, there was enough of a ... fuss about it that he was stripped of his detecting licence.'

'That must really have driven him mad, Doc! No wonder he gave me a few kicks for good measure when he was evicting me.'

'That sounds like my old PE teacher all right. Both the kicking and the ... evicting. He was mad as hell after he lost his licence, but he didn't do ... too badly out of the whole fiasco. Two of the Dalmatians had changed their wills the week before they died, and … they both left Maurice everything. Very handy for him. That's how he was able to buy up property … all over the place. Including your old flat, I suppose. And the Blue Chameleon.'

I suppose I should have been glad. I had got what I had come here for: a whole load of dirt on Maurice Masher. After all, forewarned is forearmed, and all that. Or maybe in my case, forewarned would be fourwinged. Although given how useless my two wings had been when I had my last altercation with Maurice, I didn't see what difference an extra pair would make this time around.

The problem was, Maurice Masher had more dirty secrets than a Dear Diary stuck in the middle of a pile of manure. And not only dirty secrets, but dangerous ones. I wasn't exactly relishing the prospect of interviewing a disgraced former detective and suspected triple-murder mastermind, who I had last seen physically assaulting me in order to remove me from his property.

Still, I had a case to work and he was my next step. In fact, I didn't have any other leads so he was my *only* step. I thanked Doc for his time and headed back up overground, my turkey-eyes watering as I waddled back out into the bright daylight.

My tail-feathers throbbing nervously at the prospect of another kicking, I headed off to the Blue Chameleon to meet Maurice Masher.

7

THE BLUE CHAMELEON

It has been said that an army marches on its stomach. Don't ask me who said it – I have no idea, and if you care that much about it you can look it up for yourself. Also, it's a pretty stupid thing to say unless you're talking about an army of earthworms. The rest of us march on our feet, or paws, or whatever is at the end of our legs. But I did think that a pit stop for some grub (and possibly some grubs) was in order after visiting Doc. So it was fairly late by the time I headed out to the Blue Chameleon and Maurice Masher. Little did I know at the time that I wasn't the only one who was late.

The closer I got to the Blue Chameleon, the more nervous I became. What if Maurice Masher turned violent? After all, he was probably responsible for three Dalmatians becoming dearly departed doggies, so a little bit of turkey would pose no problem for him. He'd probably eat me for lunch with extra cranberry sauce if he realised that I was trying to rake up his past in an attempt to solve my case. I supposed I could try my whole 'I rang the police before I came here' routine again, but I wasn't totally confident that it would work a second time.

As it turned out, I didn't have to worry about Maurice Masher.

The first indication I had that something was wrong was the commotion outside the club. I knew that the Blue Chameleon went in for glitz and glamour, but this was ridiculous. The whole street outside was full of flashing blue lights. It took me a few seconds to realise that they were police cars – us turkeys aren't always the quickest on the uptake. Neither are we the quickest at being quick, but I did my fastest turkey-waddle to the door of the Blue Chameleon. I suddenly had a really bad feeling about this.

I told the policemen at the entrance to the club that I was working on a case about threats to the Blue Chameleon, and this seemed to do the trick. I was rushed straight in to the crime scene, which up to half an hour ago had been Maurice Masher's office. It wasn't Maurice Masher's office any more because Maurice Masher himself was no more. 'Rest in peace, turkey-walloper,' I thought.

The man (well, the Dobermann) in charge at the crime scene was Detective Dazzer. I had come across him during my work on the Case of the Rampaging Rhino. He was very smart but also very sarcastic and a bit intimidating. He didn't suffer fools gladly – in fact, he didn't suffer fools at all.

He was still surveying the crime scene when I arrived. He cast a quick glance at me as I came in, then went back to glumly peering around the office. There was a funny smell in the room, something unpleasant that lurked behind all the everyday office smells. But before I could put my feather on what exactly it was, Dazzer spoke in his low, gravelly growl.

'I presume you have some connection to this mess that explains your presence here, Seamus.'

'Oh yes, detective. I was hired to look into possible threats to the Blue Chameleon.'

'Well, it looks like someone followed through on those threats. As you can see, the victim is almost certainly dead.'

The enormous body of my ex-landlord was sprawled across his desk. It didn't take an expert to see that he had been stabbed. The great big knife that was still sticking up from his back was a seriously big clue. If he wasn't dead, he was certainly doing a great impression of it.

'He's quite a looker, isn't he?' the detective drawled.

Boars are generally ugly creatures at the best of times, and this definitely wasn't the best of times for Maurice Masher. Although now he would almost certainly cause less damage to my behind with his vicious right boot. And speaking of damage …

'Speaking of damage …' I began.

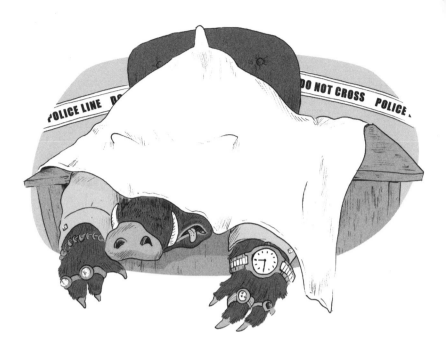

'I don't believe you were,' cut in Dazzer.

'What?'

'Damage. You weren't speaking of it, Seamus. You hadn't said much of anything at all.'

'Well, if I wasn't speaking of damage, I must have been thinking about it. Or maybe I was just thinking of thinking about it. Either way, there seems to be very little of it in the room.'

'There seems to be very little thinking in the room, is it, Seamus? I could be uncharitable and put that down to you coming in here.'

'Oh no, detective – damage. There seems to be very little damage in the room. No sign of a fight or a struggle or anything. Maybe Maurice Masher knew his attacker?'

Dazzer took a long, careful look at me. 'I was just thinking that myself, Seamus. Are there any other observations you'd like to share with me?'

'I should really speak to my client first.' I didn't want to go telling Dazzer about Miss Ermine, not until I had a chance to talk to her myself. I wasn't ready for those €100 notes to dry up yet. I had got a taste for food beyond Shredded Worms and wanted to keep on tasting it.

'You can speak to your client all you like, Seamus, but I don't think you'll get much out of him,' said the detective, nodding to the dead body.

'Oh no, Maurice Masher isn't my client.'

Dazzer looked surprised. 'So if Mr Masher here didn't hire you, then who exactly did?'

'I'd rather not say yet. For the time being, let's just say that it was ... someone with an interest in this case.'

'Well then, for the time being, let's just say that you can remove yourself from my crime scene, Seamus. When you feel like cooperating, you know where to find me. And if I find out that your interested someone had some involvement in this, you'll be in serious trouble.'

With that, I was escorted out of a club owner's office for the second time that day.

And, for the second time, the person doing the escorting was very much on the muscly side. He was another police-dog I had met during the Case of the Rampaging Rhino. However, while Detective Dazzer was a lean and razor-sharp Dobermann, my current escort was an oversized bulldog who was about as sharp as a block of cheese. Fittingly, he was called Cheddar.

As Cheddar led me out of the club, my head was full of questions. Who had killed Maurice Masher? Did Simon the Snake have anything to do with it? He had certainly seemed to know that Maurice might be in danger. And what about Imelda Ermine? Was she OK? Or was she lying face down with a stab wound in her back somewhere else in the club? Like one of those impossible maths tests that you have to sit in a nightmare, I had way too many questions and no answers at all.

We were passing one of the dressing rooms when a chair flew out the open door and crashed against the opposite wall, smashing into smithereens. I jumped and gave a fairly ungainly squawk. Cheddar, showing all the reflexes of a block of cheese, ground to a halt, looking uncertain. This flying-chair phenomenon was new to him. He was clearly not sure why the chair had decided to fly out the door and was wondering if it had friends who were going to follow close behind it. I was also stumped, until I heard a low female purr, full of menace.

'I can't believe that you could even *suggest* such a thing. I will have to take this matter up with Detective Dazzer. And when I do, I will be *sure* to mention you by name.'

It was – who else? – Imelda Ermine.

8

MORE UNUSUAL THAN USUAL

For the second time that day, I had a flash of inspiration. It must have been something to do with my improved diet of deep-fried grub-based foods.

I waddled confidently into the dressing room, ready to seize my chance to get some 'alone time' with my client.

'It's OK, Miss Ermine, I'm here now.'

Cheddar began to protest but I cut him off with a wave. 'Thank you for escorting me this far, sir. You can now resume your post at the entrance. I'll take it from here.' I'm not sure that Cheddar had ever been called 'sir' before. He seemed thrown off balance by it. I don't think he knew if it was an insult or a compliment.

'But wasn't I meant to bring *you* to the entrance, Mr Turkey, and kick you out?' Poor old Cheddar was confuddled.

'Not at all, sir. *You* were meant to go to the entrance after bringing *me* to Miss Ermine. You must have misheard your orders. An easy mistake to make, but there's no harm done. Thank you for your help. I'll be sure to commend you to Detective Dazzer.'

Cheddar hesitated for another second, then shook his squashy-nosed head and trundled away. I wasn't sure how soon he would realise his mistake so I didn't know how much time I had. But I knew I would have to be quick.

I turned back to the dressing room.

It was like a bomb site. Bottles, chairs, clothes and assorted cosmetics were everywhere. Miss Ermine had obviously thrown a strop, and when that didn't work, she had started throwing the furniture.

In the centre of the chaos stood Miss Ermine herself, her fur coat drawn tight around her shoulders and her mouth drawn tight in a furious pout. A police-dog I didn't recognise was awkwardly backed up against one wall, clearly wishing that he could escape through it.

I kept going with my super confidence, wondering how many people I would be able to fool with my bluffing before my luck ran out. 'Thank you for guarding Miss Ermine, I'll take it from here. You're needed back at the station. A gang of chimpanzees is running riot downtown and all officers are to report to base.'

Even though the poor police-dog was clearly afraid of Miss Ermine, he must have been even more afraid of Detective Dazzer. 'I was told to guard Miss Ermine until my boss is ready to talk to her.'

'Yes, but I'm here now.' I was hoping he wouldn't ask who I was – I wasn't sure what I'd say if he did. 'Your boss, Detective Dazzer, has personally ordered me to relieve you of your duty here. You are to return to base immediately. Those chimps are really causing havoc, and we need to put all the police-dogs we can get out on the streets to restore the peace.'

He looked nervously at me, stole a glance at the still-scowling cat, then shrugged just like Cheddar had done and bolted for the exit, closing the door behind him. Presumably he thought that a bunch of rampaging chimpanzees was less daunting than Miss Ermine and her airborne chairs.

Imelda Ermine continued to scowl at me for a moment, then slowly broke into a wolfish grin. 'Nicely done, Mr Turkey. You were *sooo* smooth. Although rampaging chimpanzees was maybe a little over the top.'

I had no time for pleasantries. I didn't know how long it would be before the police-dog met a fellow police-dog and figured out that the chimpanzees were simply a figment of my imagination. So I got straight down to brass tacks.

'Miss Ermine, what's been going on here? Yesterday you came to me with a problem that wasn't really a problem. Today your boss has been murdered. And I take it from the police-dog who was here that you are one of the main suspects.' I was taking an educated guess with that last bit, but I reckoned I was right. After all, what else could the police-dog have said that would have got her so worked up? And there was still something about Miss Ermine that I didn't trust. Throwing €100 notes around the place like confetti could buy you a big chunk of trust, but it still wasn't enough to make me totally at ease with her.

'Oh, Seamus, isn't it terrible? Poor Maurice, he was such a sweet dear.'

That stopped me in my tracks for a second, as I wondered if we were talking about the same person. As far as I was concerned, anyone who called Maurice Masher 'sweet' needed to have their head examined. And he was a boar, not a deer. Still, I let it pass.

'And what exactly do you know about poor Maurice's passing, Miss Ermine? Did you see anything unusual today? Or any*one* unusual, maybe?'

The cat fiddled playfully with the fine gold chain she was wearing. Whether she meant it to or not, the main effect of this was to highlight her perfectly painted, beautifully manicured and above all very, very sharp claws.

She grinned. 'A lot of the people at the Blue Chameleon are what you might call unusual.' She paused for a second, thinking, then went on. 'But there was one person who was more unusual than usual, if you catch my drift. I didn't tell the police-dog about him, as he was being *sooo* mean. But I'd be glad to tell *you*.'

I didn't catch her drift – I had no idea what 'more unusual than usual' meant – but figured that if she thought it was important then I should hear it. 'That'd be great, Miss Ermine. Do go on.'

'It was at about three o' clock, just twenty minutes before Maurice was killed. I was here in my dressing room getting ready for my afternoon performance when I heard someone in the corridor outside. I thought it was Johnny Two-Fingers – he plays the piano for me when I'm singing – so I called him. But all I heard back was a loud grunt. I don't need to tell you, Seamus, that when I call people, I don't expect to get a grunt in reply. So I called again, but all I got was another grunt.

'I had to know who it was – only the staff are allowed back here, and I couldn't have one of *them* grunting at me. But you wouldn't believe what I saw when I opened the door, Seamus – the biggest, ugliest pig I have ever seen. He gave another grunt and said something I couldn't really understand, about a meeting with Maurice – his pronunciation was just *aw*ful. And then he was gone.'

Suddenly I remembered the strange smell in Maurice Masher's office. It was the same as the smell in the Club-footed Pigeon, the smell of sweaty, farting piggy bouncers. It looked like either my old friend Snot or his buddy Booger had been lurking around the Blue Chameleon right before Maurice met his messy end.

'Did this pig have a very distinctive odour, Miss Ermine?'

'He certainly did, Seamus. A particularly *pungent* one.'

'Would you say it was like the smell of pig farts?'

'Well, I wouldn't consider myself an expert on the farting habits of rude ugly pigs, but it certainly was a very *smelly* smell. I had to spray half a bottle of Eau de Nip du Chat in the hall to mask it. It was *highly* unpleasant.'

'And did this pig have a lot of piercings?'

'Oh yes – his ears, his nose, his lip, even his knuckles. And I thought they were just bone, so I don't know *how* you'd pierce them. By drilling, I suppose.'

Well, the pierced knuckles made all the difference. It had to be Booger. I had noticed them right after I'd noticed the size, the smell and the slowness.

We had ourselves a brand new lead suspect.

'Thank you, Miss Ermine. You've been most helpful. I'm going to have to go now and have a chat with Detective Dazzer about all of this and clear your name.'

'Do you think that you could do that, Seamus? All I want is to bring *poor* Maurice to justice.'

'Don't you mean bring his killer to justice?'

'Oh yes, of course. *Silly* me.'

'Right so. I'll go talk to Dazzer. It shouldn't take more than half an hour to get this mess straightened out.'

9

THE LONG WALK HOME

As I was splashing back to my office through torrential rain two hours later, my outlook on life in general, and on this case in particular, was an awful lot less sunny.

Partly this was due to the weather. The rain was so heavy it threatened to strip paint from walls and give small animals serious concussion. I still had most of the cat's money, enough to pay for a helicopter ride back to the office, not to mind a taxi. Unfortunately, it was all currently stashed *in* the office, so I couldn't use it to get me back *to* the office.

And partly it was due to Detective Dazzer's reaction to my news about Booger. When I went back to see him after talking to Imelda Ermine, I didn't expect to get a big sloppy Dobermann kiss or a bouquet of flowers or a huge cake and a rendition of 'For He's a Jolly Good Fellow'. But he could have said 'Great job' or 'Nicely done' or something to that effect. Or, if he was feeling

especially generous, 'Excellent work, Seamus. Here, take this solid gold statue from Maurice Masher's desk in recognition of your super sleuthing and to help make up for all the kickings he gave you when he was alive.' But no, the conversation unfolded along these lines:

Me: Detective Dazzer, I have some information that you might find useful in your investigation.

Dazzer: [*Grumpily.*] I thought you had been escorted off the premises.

Me: Well, almost.

Dazzer: Almost? Almost, as in not at all?

Me: Well, yes. But I did find out there was a highly suspicious character lurking around the Blue Chameleon just before Maurice was killed.

Dazzer: Right. [*Grumpy pause where Dazzer didn't want to ask me who it was even though he was dying to because he was still grumpy with me for not leaving. But then he asked anyway.*] Well, spit it out. Who was it?

Me: One of the bouncers from the Clubfooted Pigeon. His name is Booger.

Dazzer: And your source for this nugget of gossip is?

Me: Imelda Ermine. She's a singer here at the club.

Dazzer: [*Now very peeved off.*] I know *exactly* who Imelda Ermine is. And she identified this bouncer, this Booger?

Me: Well, no, she saw him and she described him to me. But I was at the Clubfooted Pigeon today and I recognised him from her description.

Dazzer: I take it that Miss Ermine is your client, then?

Me: [*A bit embarrassed.*] Yeah, she is. She was worried about threats to the Blue Chameleon, threats coming from the Clubfooted Pigeon. That's why I was down there earlier.

Dazzer: Sounds like you had quite a busy day.

Me: Well, when I was down there earlier I met Simon, the owner. [*In fairness, Dazzer did look impressed by this. Simon was a pretty hard guy to meet. Especially if you wanted to leave the meeting all in one piece and still breathing.*] That's when I saw Booger. And talked to him too. Though I didn't get much in the way of replies. He's probably still processing my questions. Then I stopped in for some barbecued bugs on the way to the Blue Chameleon, which I guess is why I didn't see Booger here. He was here around three o'clock, and Maurice bit the dust at about 3.20. So that has to make Booger the number one suspect.

Dazzer: [*Looking startled.*] How do you know what time Maurice died?

Me: Imelda Ermine. She told me that Booger was here around three, about twenty minutes before Maurice was killed. I did the maths myself – it wasn't that hard really – and figured out that he must have kicked the bucket at 3.20. Elementary.

Detective Dazzer looked at me very strangely, as if he had just realised that I had six legs and wasn't sure if he should be worried about this or really, really angry. In the end, he settled for being serious and concerned.

Dazzer: All right, Seamus, you're a nice turkey. So I'm going to give you some advice. Stay out of this. All of this. Whatever you have to tell Miss Ermine in order to do that, whatever story you have to spin, spin it. Drop this case. Get out and stay out. It'll only mean trouble for you if you don't. Imelda Ermine, Booger, Simon, these are all serious people who mean serious business. If you're in any doubt about the kind of business they are in, or just how serious they are about it, look at what happened to Maurice Masher. He's a very powerful guy in this town, with a lot of money and a lot of muscle. Well, he *was* all of those things. Now he's getting colder and uglier by the hour. If that can happen to Maurice, with all that power and all that money, imagine what could happen to you.

And that was it. With a curt nod, Dazzer turned away. Two police-dogs who had come up behind me during the exchange gently but firmly took hold of my wings and steered me out of the building and onto the street. Though now, instead of a street, it was more like a roaring torrent.

A good day for ducks, but a bad one for turkeys.

I was still mulling over all of this when I arrived at my office. It's not easy to open doors using your wings at the best of times, and this was the wettest rather than the best of times. After an age of fiddling with my numb and bedraggled wings, I managed to get the key in the lock and the front door opened.

I sighed with relief as I stepped into the quiet, dark and above all *dry* hallway.

Then I stopped.

Apart from the front door, there are three doors off the hallway: one to the bathroom, one to the broom closet and the third to my office. The first two doors were masked in darkness, but a sliver of light showed under the third.

'That's odd,' I thought. 'I don't remember leaving that light on.'

Then I heard a muffled noise from the office. The muffled noise of someone who was trying to be very quiet but had just knocked over a very large stack of dirty bowls.

There was someone in my office.

10

AN UNINVITED GUEST

A turkey has a resting heart rate of roughly a hundred and
ninety-three beats per minute. Given all of the walking
I'd been doing, the stressful nature of my day and the seriously unhealthy diet I had had for the last few weeks, my
heart rate was probably up around three hundred bpm as
I fumbled with the key and opened the front door. When
I realised that there was someone in the office, I'd say it
rocketed to over a thousand. At least. It was beating so
hard I thought I was going to crack a rib. I probably set a
new Turkey Heart Rate World Record.

Still, as my business cards said, I was a turkey, not a
chicken. And I had no way to call the police. If you've
never tried to use a mobile phone with feathers instead
of fingers, take my advice: don't. So I reckoned it was up
to me to figure out who this intruder was.

Once I got my heart rate down to a relatively restful
five hundred bpm, my first thought was: maybe it's
Auntie Et. Unfortunately, thought number two was that
Auntie Et had an amazing knack of never knocking

over any of the dirty bowls, plates and cups in the office, no matter how messy and cluttered it got, so thought number one had to be scrapped.

My heart going like a jackhammer again – about as fast and nearly as loud – I sidled up to the office door and pressed my ear to it. I could hear someone inside moving around slowly, opening cupboards and rummaging around in them. They were clearly searching for something, though I had no idea what. What could I possibly have that someone would want? The cat's money was cunningly hidden in the cistern of the toilet, so if that was what they were looking for then we could be here all night. Apart from that, I really had nothing worth taking.

It suddenly occurred to me that I had no plan here. I couldn't very well barge into the room. What if it was someone like Snot or Booger? I'd be following Maurice Masher into the great petting zoo in the sky faster than you could say 'Lucky turkey's mucky loo key.' I had come into the hallway unnoticed. It was unlikely that I would be able to get into the office unnoticed. Turkeys are built to waddle, not to tiptoe.

I was just assessing my options when I heard the intruder say something that sounded awfully like 'Aha!' and give a little chuckle. Which was bad news for me on two counts. The little chuckle meant that it definitely couldn't be Auntie Et – she never laughed, ever. And the 'Aha!' sounded like the intruder had found what they'd been looking for and was about to leave the office. By opening the door that my ear was currently pressed up against.

I had to act quickly. With all the speed of a turkey that has been invited to Christmas dinner and knows that it is going to be on the menu, I dived down the hallway, yanked open the door to the broom closet and ducked inside. I left the door open just a crack – having gone through all of this stress, I was determined to get a look at who had broken in.

A second later the door to the office swung open and light from inside flooded out into the hallway. Luckily none of it fell on me, my eye pressed to the crack in the door of the broom closet. 'C'mon!' I thought. 'Let's get a good look at you!' The intruder, however, had other plans. As suddenly as the door had swung open, the light of the office was switched off and the hallway was plunged into complete darkness.

I think I gave a little gasp – I'm not sure. I definitely felt like giving a little gasp, or even a big huge gasp. It was so dark I couldn't see my feathers in front of my face. My heart started up again with its hyperactive *thump-thump-thump-thump-thump*. Other than that, the hallway seemed totally silent.

'This is not good,' I thought after a few seconds. 'If the intruder was going to just leave, I would have heard the front door opening by now.' But there was no sign of that or any other movement. Which meant they were still here, in the pitch black.

Silence.

And then,

verrry slowly,

the bathroom door squeeeaked open.

'Why are they opening the bathroom door?' I thought. 'Surely they aren't going to use the toilet in the middle of a burglary?' And then, more urgently, I thought: 'Oh no! The intruder knows that someone is here and is looking for them!' I felt a cold sweat break out on my face. The inside of my beak felt dry. The broom closet – my makeshift hiding place – was the only place left for them to look. The next *squeeeak* would be for me.

More silence.

As if by itself, I felt my wing close around the handle of the mop. Needless to say, it had never closed around the handle of the mop before. I'm not really a mopping-the-floor kind of person – I'm more of a cover-the-floor-with-dirty-clothes-and-dishes kind of person. At that moment, though, it seemed like the best thing in the broom closet with which to defend myself. 'If I don't have to use you on the intruder,' I whispered in my head to the mop, 'I promise I will use you every day to clean the floor. Well, at least once a week. Or definitely once anyway. Or at the very least I'll definitely take you out of the broom closet and into the office. Although that might just upset you, when you see the state of it.'

My mental bargaining with the mop was interrupted by another squeak. This one was quieter than the first, but an awful lot closer. It was still pitch black, but the intruder must have opened the door of the broom closet.

'Oh God,' I thought, 'this is it. And I'll never even get to see who it is.'

In the next instant, a lot of things happened at the same time. Or at least very quickly, one after the other. It was hard to keep track of them at the time.

There was a muffled banging on the front door and someone shouted, 'Seamus! Are you home?'

I gave a yell and swung the mop at where I guessed the intruder was. It was still pitch black, but I definitely felt the mop hit someone. Unfortunately, it wasn't a proper wallop, but it did enough to give them a shock. There was a yelp, and I was shoved back into the broom closet along with the mop. I heard a door slam, then the smashing of a lot of dishes as the intruder made their way through the office with a lot more haste and less care than earlier. Finally, there was one very loud and very final-sounding crash.

It took me a few seconds to untangle myself from the mop and exit the closet. The banging at the front door had got louder and was now accompanied by shouts of 'Open up! This is the police!' Clearly they had heard the commotion and getting in had suddenly become a lot more urgent for them. I fumbled for the light switch and got the front door open as quickly as I could.

'There's an intruder!' I gestured wildly at the now-closed office door. 'They were in my office when I came home, and they've gone back in there!'

'Were they armed?' It was Cheddar, along with the police-dog from Imelda Ermine's dressing room.

'I don't know. I heard you at the door and I hit them with the mop, and then they ran into the office. But it was dark, so I didn't see them.'

'All right, turkey. We'll take it from here.'

Cheddar and his colleague squared up to the office door. They looked at each other for a second, then nodded and burst into the room shouting, 'Police! Don't move!'

I peered in around the door.

Smashed dishes littered the floor. The doors of all the cupboards hung open.

Rain pelted in through the broken window.

The intruder was gone.

11

SECOND THOUGHTS

I hardly slept at all that night, and when I did I had the same terrible dream, over and over again. I dreamt that a giant nose was chasing me through endless corridors, bouncing along behind me and laughing evilly. Eventually it got me cornered and swallowed me up in one of its nostrils. Inside the nostril, Snot and Booger were waiting for me. They plucked me and shoved me into a huge pot with carrots, onions and an old boot. When they threw cold water into the pot with me, I woke up with a splutter.

Each time I woke the sheet of plastic I had taped over the broken window had fallen down, and rain was once again pelting into the office. I taped the plastic back up, went back to sleep and had the same dream all over again.

After the fourth time around I had had enough of Snot, Booger, the giant nose and being rained on, so I went to sleep in the broom closet, hugging the mop to my chest like it was my favourite teddy bear. I slept much better there and didn't wake until Auntie Et arrived in

the morning to find the office in an even worse state of repair than usual.

I filled her in on what had happened. It turned out that Detective Dazzer had asked Cheddar and his colleague (named Stilton) to call around to my office and make sure that I was OK. Which turned out to be very lucky for me, as they arrived just in time to save my bacon (as it were) from the intruder. They were also supposed to urge me to drop Imelda Ermine's case, if it wasn't already too late. This time I was much more receptive to the idea. After the break-in I was having serious second thoughts about this case, and this whole detecting business in general. I'd agreed to call to the police station in the morning to give a statement about the break-in.

Auntie Et listened to all of this with a cranky look on her face, then simply said, 'What did you expect, hmmm, taking on this case? Never trust a cat who wears a fur coat. You never know who it's been.'

Whatever I had expected taking on this case, I clearly shouldn't have expected any sympathy at all from Auntie Et. So, leaving her even more grumpy looking than ever in the damp wreckage of the office, I headed towards the police station for my date with the doggy duo.

As usual, however, my stomach got the better of me. Halfway to the station, I found myself powerless to resist the call of the deep-fried grub ball, so I ducked into Greasy Gertie's for a quick fill-me-up. As I slunk guiltily through the door, I told myself that I would only have one helping of deep-fried grub balls. And then that I deserved a second helping after the night I'd had, and they were really small helpings anyway, and I could do with fattening up. After all, no-one likes a scrawny turkey. And then I told myself that I mightn't get to eat lunch – after all, the life of a private detective had suddenly become much more exciting, and you never knew what would happen next – so I should really have a third helping. Just in case.

I was just about to tuck into my fourth helping ('There could be a worldwide shortage of deep-fried grub balls tomorrow, and then I'd regret only having three helpings today') when I heard the news headlines on the radio. Well, I heard the first one. After that, everything was a blur for a few minutes.

Following the untimely passing of Maurice Masher, the owner of the Blue Chameleon, yesterday, police are reporting today that the owner of the Clubfooted Pigeon, first name Simon, last name unknown, has also passed away. The two clubs were in fierce competition, but police are not yet saying if there is a connection between the two events. In other news, Dopey the Dolphin was found with his fins …

I didn't hear what else he had to say about Dopey or any other news. My head was spinning. This was really bad.

First Maurice Masher had been bumped off, and now the same thing had happened to Simon the Snake. Whatever the police were saying, I knew there had to be a connection between the two. I could feel it in my giblets.

But who could be behind this? Booger was the most likely suspect for Maurice's murder, but he was hardly acting on his own. He had the brawn, but not the brains. I had thought that he'd been getting orders from Simon, but if he was, then who was responsible for Simon's untimely end? Booger would hardly have done it, would he? And how did Imelda Ermine fit into this? I had more questions than ever before.

I had to get to the police station, quick. After all, I could have been added to the body count last night if Cheddar and Stilton hadn't turned up when they did. I might still be in danger, though I didn't really understand why or from whom. I gathered up the fourth helping of deep-fried grub balls to bring with me and headed for the door.

Cheddar was at the desk when I got to the station. He looked grumpy, but relieved to see me. 'We were expecting you earlier, turkey.'

'I know, I slept in. Sorry about that. Thanks again for calling over last night. You really saved my bacon. As it were.'

'We had orders to call. You can thank the orders.'

'Well, you, the orders, whoever: thanks. And I heard this morning that the owner of the Clubfooted Pigeon died. Is it true?'

Cheddar frowned. 'It is all right.'

'Well, then I'm doubly glad you arrived last night when you did. I could easily have been victim number three if you hadn't.'

'Sit down there, turkey,' said Cheddar, pointing to a chair facing his desk, 'and we'll get started.'

I sat.

'You know, it's funny you mentioned the owner of the Clubfooted Pigeon,' he said, and from out of nowhere he slapped a pair of handcuffs on my wings. 'I'm placing you under arrest for his murder.'

12

ELVIS KNIGHT

I couldn't believe it. I was behind bars.

I could just imagine the look on Auntie Et's face. It would probably be her usual grumpy look, with an extra dash of ferocious-hyena-disapproval and a side order of I-told-you-so. Maybe it would be better to stay behind bars for good, so I wouldn't have to deal with her.

What's more, I wasn't even able to feel sorry for myself in peace. I had a very talkative cellmate, a meerkat who just wouldn't stop smiling. Or winking. And she chattered incessantly.

'So, Seamus!' *Wink wink.* 'You're innocent, is it?' *Wink wink.* 'Course you are!' *Wink wink.* 'We're all innocent here!'

I wasn't sure if the wink was because she was joking or because she had something stuck in her eye. Or maybe it was because she had something stuck in her brain. Whatever the reason, if she didn't put a stop to it soon there was a good chance *I* was going to stick something in her brain myself.

'Eh, well, actually, I *am* innocent. There must have been some kind of mistake.'

'Or you've been framed, kiddo!' *Wink wink.*

This hadn't occurred to me before, but now that she mentioned it, it was a definite possibility. I was beginning to wonder who might have been behind it, when she continued on like a demented conversational steamroller. I couldn't concentrate enough on my own thoughts so I just gave up and listened to her.

'It can happen to the best of us!' *Wink wink.* 'Sometimes it even happens to pictures! And they don't hurt anyone!' *Wink wink, chortle chortle.* 'Unless they fall on your head!'

'But why would anyone want to frame me? What did *I* ever do?'

'It's not what you did, kiddo!' *Wink wink.* 'It's what the sniffers think they can pin on you!' *Wink wink.*

'The sniffers?'

'Sure! Call them what you like: the cops, the fuzz, the police. They're all just sniffers to me!' *Wink wink.*

'But why would the police want to pin something on me? I didn't do anything!'

'The donkey didn't do anything either, but everyone wants to pin the tail on her anyway!' *Wink wink, chortle chortle.*

'So I'm a donkey now?' All of the winking was distracting me and making me lose the thread of the conversation.

'No, you goose, you're a turkey! And I'm Elvis, by the way. Elvis Knight.'

'Um, isn't Elvis a strange name for, you know …?' I trailed off awkwardly.

'For what, kiddo? For a meerkat? It's a family name! I'm the fifth Elvis in a row!'

'No, I meant more that it's a strange name for a, well, for a woman.'

Elvis laughed. 'The four Elvises before me were fellas all right, kiddo, but my mum thought it would be a

shame to ruin a family tradition, so she just went and called me Elvis too!' *Wink wink.* 'Anyway, anything that helps to throw people off the scent is fine by me. Keep them guessing, I say – if they think they're looking for a fella, they'll hardly think to look twice at me!'

'But who would be looking?'

'Anyone who I don't want finding me, kiddo!' *Wink wink.* 'The sniffers, people I owe money to, anyone I don't want to meet!'

'I suppose the sniffers – I mean, the police – finally caught up with you this time, though. And with me – though I'm still not sure how that happened. I wasn't even running away from them.'

'Don't get your tail-feathers in a twist, turkey!' *Wink wink.* 'I've got a plan to get you out of here!' *Wink wink.*

'Really? You can get me out of here? I don't know what to say, Elvis – that'd be super!'

'Sure, kid!' *Wink wink.* 'Stick with me and you'll be out of here in no time!' *Wink wink.*

I had to get this winking cleared up. It was wrecking my head, and I'd had about as much of it as I could take.

'OK, Elvis, I'm very grateful that you're going to help me get out of here, but I have to ask you, what's the story with the winking? It's driving me nuts. Are you winking because you're joking? If you are, it's a pretty bad joke to tell me you can break me out of here when actually you can't. So can you stop winking for a second and tell me straight up: can we get out of here?'

Elvis's face fell. She looked like a puppy who had been kicked. I didn't know that a meerkat's eyes could look that big and sad and teary. Suddenly I began to feel a little sorry for my mini freak-out.

'Unless, uh, you can't stop winking. If it's a condition or something that you have. I mean, I didn't want to hurt your feelings. I've just never been in jail before, and I'm a little stressed out right now. Actually, I'm a lot stressed out right now.'

Elvis perked up a little. 'Don't worry, kiddo, I'll get you out all right. You're gonna go tonight! I heard from a buddy of mine that a turkey would be joining me today. He asked me to stick around and help this turkey out with a few things – break him out of this joint, keep him out of the clutches of the cops once I got him out, help him clear his name, that kind of thing. Well, I owe this buddy of mine more than a few favours, so I figured, what the hell, it'd be fun!'

Now I felt really bad for my mini freak-out.

'As for the winking, kiddo, I just do it for the craic – it's a bit of a laugh, y'know? Things can get pretty boring in jail – you have to find some way to entertain yourself! Sometimes I put on a limp or pretend I'm from Jamaica. You want to see my Bob Marley impression?'

I really, really didn't.

'I'd love to, Elvis, but first you might explain what's going on here. Who's your friend? How did he know I was going to be arrested? And how are you going to break me out of here tonight?' Then, as an afterthought, 'Also, how many times have you been in jail?'

'The last one's easy: twenty-six times! I've never been in for more than a few days though. They've never been able to pin the tail on this donkey!' *Wink wink.*

I let that wink go, as she was going to break me out of there, but I didn't think I'd be able to take many more of them. 'So how come you're constantly being brought in here? Twenty-six times seems like an awful lot. What do you *do*? Or do I really want to know?'

'Me, kiddo? I don't do anything! At least, nothing they can prove. The only thing I'm guilty of is being a model businesswoman!' Elvis spread her paws as wide as her grin and winked again. 'Though the cops have got it into their heads that I'm somehow involved any time there's a major heist in this town, and they arrest me and dump me in here. But they've never been able to find any evidence, so they always have to let me go!'

She beamed. If her smile got any wider, I thought the top half of her head would fall off.

'All right, Elvis, so there's no evidence of you being involved in any of these heists. But if you *were* going to get involved, what would you do? The break-in? The getaway? Selling the stolen goods afterwards?'

'Well, kiddo, I do have a knack for getting into tricky places and getting out of sticky situations, and at just the right time too. But breaking the law? That's no job for an upstanding businesswoman like myself!' *Wink wink.*

Wow. I was in jail and was about to be broken out by some kind of break-in-and-break-out-again criminal mastermind. They hadn't told us that this might happen when we were in detecting school.

'So how does this work? What's the plan? And how am I going to clear my name while I'm on the run from the police?'

'You sure ask a lot of questions for a turkey. Most of them just go around saying "gobble gobble" and fattening themselves up for Christmas. Anyway, you'll probably be questioned this afternoon by the cops – just keep it together and don't say too much, and you'll be out of here once it's dark. I'll be walking out of here tomorrow morning anyway when they realise that, once again, they don't have any actual evidence against me. So there's no need for me to break out with you tonight, kiddo. I'll just stay here and make myself comfy instead.'

'But if you're staying in here tonight, how am I going to get out? And where will I go when I do? I'm rubbish at hide-and-seek, not to mind hide-while-the-police-seek.'

'Don't worry kiddo, it'll all be sorted. You'll see. After all, surely you trust a model businesswoman like myself?' *Wink wink.*

As far as I could see, if I wanted to get out of jail and clear my name, I didn't really have a choice.

13

THE CAT-DONKEY

It was a small police station, so there wasn't a full-time interrogation room. Instead Stilton and Cheddar had brought me to what appeared to be an all-purpose canteen that was used for whatever was needed: eating doughnuts, watching movies, playing marathon sessions of Twister, interrogating suspects. It looked like it had been most recently used to host a birthday party. Unwashed plates with bits of birthday cake and candles were piled up by the sink. It made me feel a little bit more at home in my new surroundings.

'Whose birthday was it?' I asked cheerily. 'Hope they had a fantastic day!'

'None of your business,' Cheddar grunted. 'Sit down and shut up.'

I shut up. I sat down. It was in the wrong order, but I didn't think Cheddar would mind.

The rest of the interview between myself, Stilton, and Cheddar went something like this:

Cheddar: Tell us why you murdered that snake last night.

Me: I didn't murder Simon. I was at home all night. You saw me there. There's been some kind of misunderstanding here, guys.

Cheddar: We saw you there at 10 PM. We didn't see where you went afterwards.

Me: I didn't go anywhere afterwards. I went to sleep in the office.

Cheddar: And you didn't leave all night?

Me: *Well ...* I did leave the office around 4 AM.

Stilton: Ha! So you admit you left the office in the middle of the night?

Me: Yeah, but only to go sleep in the broom closet. The rain kept coming in the broken window.

Cheddar: Well, can you explain how a pair of shears belonging to you was found at the murder scene?

Me: [*Stunned.*] Um, no. I can't. I have no idea how that happened.

Cheddar: Those shears were used to kill Simon. And they have your business card taped to them with a note saying: 'Please return to Seamus the Shamus if found. Thank ewe!' [*Smiling at how smart he was.*] Pretty sloppy work there, turkey.

I couldn't figure out what was going on at all. Then it hit me.

Me: Of course! They're the not-too-rusty shears I keep in the bottom drawer of my office desk. The ones I use to fleece my sheepish customers, when required. The intruder must have stolen them when he broke in last night!

Cheddar: I'm glad you mentioned the intruder. Did you manage to get a good look at him?

Me: No, I told you. It was dark when he was in the hall, and by the time you two got into the office, he was gone.

Stilton: That's what you say.

Me: [*Confused.*] Well, yes, it is. That's because it's what happened.

Stilton:	[*Sticking to his guns.*] That's what you say.
Me:	[*Getting frustrated.*] OK, this isn't helping. [*To Cheddar.*] Is he stuck on Repeat or something?
Cheddar:	Well, we saw no intruder. When you let us in, the light was on in the hallway, your office was empty and the window was broken. How do we know there even *was* an intruder?
Me:	Of course there was an intruder! Why would I have trashed my own office and broken my own window? I got soaked last night because of it and had terrible dreams about a giant jumping killer nose!
Cheddar:	[*Smiling like the cat who got the cream.*] You'd have done it so you could have a perfect alibi.

This was not going well. Then it started going a whole lot worse.

Cheddar:	We also know that you had a motive. We had a call from your client, Miss Ermine, this morning. She heard that Simon had been killed and was very upset. She said that she had offered you a €1,000 bonus if you 'took care of' the Clubfooted Pigeon. Permanently. She thought that maybe you had read more into that than you should

	have. She was very upset to think that she might have been the cause of this.
Me:	What? No! I mean, yeah, I think she said something like that, but I'd never, you know. I mean, really, I'm a turkey! Whoever heard of a turkey murdering anyone?
Cheddar:	[*Grimly.*] There's a first time for everything. Anyway, you could be one of those psycho turkeys.
Me:	What psycho turkeys? What are you talking about? There are no psycho turkeys!
Stilton:	That's what you say.
Me:	This is crazy, I never killed anyone!
Cheddar:	Like I said, there's a first time for everything.
Me:	Maybe, but I'm telling you this isn't it!
Stilton:	That's what you say.

I thought I was going to cry. I had assumed that once I talked to the police, they would see that I was innocent. Instead this was turning into a nightmare. And I wished Stilton would stop saying that.

Cheddar:	I also have to tell you that you are now the lead suspect in the murder of Maurice Masher.
Me:	What?! No way. I didn't arrive at the Blue Chameleon until way after he was killed!

He was killed at 3.20. I was stuffing my face at that stage.

Cheddar: How do you know he was killed at 3.20?

Me: I don't know. No, wait, Imelda Ermine told me.

Cheddar: She couldn't have. When we talked to her, she had no idea what time Maurice Masher was killed. We thought the time of death was around 3.15, but we never told anyone that. We told the reporters that he died around five, so that's what was on the news. You're the only person we talked to who knew the time of death. Now how do you explain that?

Me: Imelda Ermine! She told me! How else would I know?

Stilton: You'd know if *you* killed him.

Me: But I didn't! Besides, Imelda Ermine said she saw that bouncer, Booger, from the Clubfooted Pigeon, sneaking around the Blue Chameleon at about three o' clock.

Cheddar: We asked her about that too. Miss Ermine told us that she never saw any pig. She has no idea what you're talking about.

Me: She must be lying! She told me that she saw him! Have you checked up on where he was yesterday?

Cheddar: Of course we have. What do you think we are, amateurs? Booger was working at the Clubfooted Pigeon all afternoon. The other bouncer working with him vouched for him – Bunk is his name.

Me: Don't you mean Snot?

Cheddar: Nope, Bunk. Snot had the afternoon off to visit his granny. I guess there must be someone in the world who loves him.

This was crazy. Had Imelda Ermine suddenly got amnesia?

Then a much more disturbing thought occurred to me: was Imelda Ermine actually involved in these murders and now trying to frame me for them? I had no idea what was going on, but I was going to need Elvis Knight's help if I was going to clear my name and pin the tail on the guilty donkey.

Even if that guilty donkey was a cat.

14

THE DISAPPEARING TRICK

It was night by the time I was brought back to the cell. Unfortunately, the police station appeared to have a lights-out-and-early-to-bed policy, with no bedtime story or soothing cup of hot chocolate on offer for the inmates.

Elvis was hopping around the cell with excitement when I was shoved back into it. She was so worked up I thought that either she would have a heart attack or her head would explode. Luckily for both of us, neither happened. Turkeys aren't good at giving mouth-to-mouth resuscitation – beaks aren't really made for it – so we're not much use if someone has a heart attack. And if someone's head explodes, well, nothing is any use except for a good mop and bucket. And I think I've already mentioned that I'm fairly useless in the cleaning-up department. So it was a lucky escape on both counts.

Thankfully, once the police-dog who was on night duty had wandered off to watch reruns of *Gopher the Gremlin*, Elvis was able to share her good news with me.

'OK, kiddo, this is it! You're definitely gonna break out of this joint tonight! Another five minutes I'd say and you'll be on your way out of here. I can't wait!' She gave an extra big wink – just one on its own this time. 'And while you were off being grilled and roasted by Tweedledum and Tweedledummer, I managed to swipe this!'

She beamed as she held up a very expensive-looking locket on a gold chain. I had been planning to fill her in on my problems with Cheddar and Stilton, but this threw me off track.

'Where did you get that?' It looked vaguely familiar.

'I heard them talking about it earlier! It was one of the pieces of evidence they took from your office – I think it was tangled up in a broom or something, and they thought it looked very out of place. I reckon they were going to charge you with stealing it, so I figured I'd nick it myself to keep you out of trouble. They'll have a hard time charging you with stealing it if they don't have it! And I reckon it's worth quite a bit – it's solid gold, y'know. So, two birds with one stone, kiddo! Not that I'm in favour of killing birds or anything, Mister Turkey!'

It was dark in the cell so I couldn't see the locket clearly, and I was still all up in a heap after my interrogation. But I had definitely seen that locket before. I just couldn't put my feather on exactly where or when.

What I was sure of, though, was that I didn't want to be in any more trouble than I was already. 'Elvis, you have to put it back. They only suspect me of stealing it at the moment. They'll *know* that I stole it if you take it now.'

That took some of the air out of her. She frowned. She pouted. She looked sulky, like a child who's been told that everyone is having cake except for her.

Thankfully, before she could start complaining or stamping her foot, there was a tap on the floor. Or rather, there was a tap from *underneath* the floor.

Elvis perked up a little. 'Hmm. Well, we'll talk about that later, kiddo. Right now, we need to get you out of here! This is what I like to call the Disappearing Trick. Come on, give me a hand. Or a wing.'

She motioned me over, and we pushed the bed away from the wall. There was another tap – I could hear that it came from one of the floor tiles. With a wink, Elvis pulled a mini crowbar out from somewhere on her person. Clearly she was better at hiding things than the police were at finding them. I wondered what else she had stashed away.

She prised the tile up from the floor to reveal a dark hole and, with a theatrical flourish, said, 'Voila! Your yellow-brick road out of here, kiddo!'

I couldn't see anything in the hole — it was almost pitch black. Also, as I may have already mentioned, turkeys have terrible night vision. After all, we generally don't need it. Usually the most exciting things we get up to at night are sleeping, dribbling and snoring.

Then I heard a familiar voice float up from the blackness. A familiar *moley* voice. It was Doc!

'Hello there, Seamus. It's good to … see you again! I know you probably can't see me, but … Elvis will give you a hand into the hole. I have a tunnel here that we can … use to get you out of here.'

Elvis gave me a thumbs-up. 'This is it, kiddo! Here, let me grab a wing and I'll lower you down!'

Obediently I stuck out a wing. Elvis grabbed hold of it, then helped me clamber into the hole. I was dangling in the darkness, my legs flailing around for a foothold or anything solid at all. I heard Doc's voice from below me. A good bit below me.

'OK, Seamus, you just need to drop down, and we can get … out of here. It's just like when you were in detecting school, in PE class. Try to roll when you … hit the ground. That way it shouldn't hurt … too much.'

This was definitely *not* like PE class, or at least not like what *I* did in PE class. I remember rolling on the ground all right, but it was only to find a more comfortable spot when I was having a snooze. I think I might have mentioned that I used PE class to catch up on my beauty sleep. Come to think of it, I must have been the best-looking turkey in detecting school – I spent more time getting my beauty sleep than doing anything else. For the first time in my life, I was beginning to regret this.

I looked up at Elvis. 'Any chance you could lower me down a bit further? Or maybe get a sheet off the bed and lower me down on it? It still seems like an awfully long way down to Doc from here.'

I saw the bright gleam of Elvis's teeth in the gloom of the cell above me. She was grinning. 'Sorry, kiddo, no can do! I think I hear the sniffer coming back, so I'm going to have to vamoose. And anyway, everyone knows that the whole turkeys-can't-fly thing is just a myth spread by jealous chickens!'

'But I'm not ready to let go yet!' I shouted up.

The disembodied grin above me broadened. 'That's OK, kiddo, you don't have to be. I am!' With that, Elvis let go of my wing.

For a second I thought I was flying.

Then I realised that this was just wishful thinking — I'd need a good run up, a strong updraft and about a month of training.

Then I realised that I was falling, and getting faster.

Then my realising was rudely interrupted as I hit the ground with a *thud* and a loud squawk.

Once the shock of it wore off, I was surprised that I wasn't hurt more. The ground seemed remarkably soft. And furry.

As Elvis heaved the tile back in place up above my head, I heard her call down: 'Bullseye! Great disappearing trick, kiddo! I can't wait to see the guard's face in the morning!' Her chuckle was cut off by the tile falling back into place with a dull *thunk*. So too was the light.

Then I felt the ground beneath me stir, and I heard Doc's voice, kind of muffled. 'It's great to bump into you ... again so soon, Seamus, but would you ... mind moving off me? I'm beginning to have ... difficulty breathing. And seeing. You're sitting on ... my head.'

15

THE LONG CRAWL TO FREEDOM

I scrambled off Doc, apologising profusely until he shushed me. 'That's fine, Seamus. Elvis was aiming for me. I know what you were like in PE class, so I thought you'd … injure yourself if you had to land on the ground. I was planning to … catch you, but I think I overestimated my … catching ability. And I underestimated your … size. Anyway, we'd better get going.' He flicked on a torch. 'This way.'

Off he went down a narrow tunnel. I kept as close behind him as I could. There were tunnels leading off to right and left as we went, and occasionally Doc would turn down one of these. I didn't want to get lost down here.

Some animals are born to crawl. Moles, for one. And baby humans. And creepy crawlies. Other animals have crawling thrust upon them and aren't too happy about it. Turkeys fall into this category. We aren't built for crawling. Our knees bend the wrong way for it. But

I gave it my best shot. Awkward crawling was preferable to being stuck down here forever.

The sides of the tunnel were earth, with wooden struts every few feet that presumably kept the tunnels from collapsing. Every so often I would catch a glimpse of a worm or grub wriggling around in the tunnel wall, looking slightly lost and extremely delicious. But I was more worried about losing Doc than I was about snacking, so I apologised to my belly and crawled on.

'Hey, Doc,' I called, 'is there any danger that these tunnels will fall in?'

Doc spun around. Or at least he turned around as quickly as a mole can turn. 'Not a chance. I built these tunnels myself. Mole-built tunnels don't ... collapse. Not unless someone collapses them. And the only person I know who did something like that is ... dead now. Stabbed ... in the back.'

'Wow. Rough way to go. Just like Maurice Masher.'

'Maurice Masher is who I'm talking about, Seamus. Remember I told you about the Case of the ... Disappearing Dalmatians? Well, those Dalmatians were engineers working in ... tunnels. Just like these. Then, mysteriously, there was an ... accident. An explosion of some kind. A tunnel collapsed and the Dalmatians were ... buried alive.'

I was sure I'd heard something about this before, and not just from Doc. But Doc kept speaking, and turkeys aren't great at doing more than one thing at a time, so I listened to him rather than trying to remember where I had heard about the buried-alive Dalmatians before.

'As I said, there was never enough evidence to prove that … Maurice did it. But I'm sure he did. Call it instinct. Or gut feeling. Anyway, now he's got what … he deserved.'

'And now I've been framed for it, Doc! And I wasn't even in the Blue Chameleon when it happened.'

'So I've heard, Seamus, so I've heard. Well, we'll get you somewhere safe first and out of the way of the … police. Then we'll see how we're going to … clear your name.'

'OK, Doc. By the way, how do you know Elvis?'

Doc smiled. 'Me and Elvis go way back. She's a very nice person, if you overlook her habit of … sometimes ignoring the difference between … what's hers and what's not. She's helped me out of a jam a couple of times. And I've helped her out of a few of her own. You're not the first person who's done this … disappearing trick. Elvis has done it a few times herself. Anyway, enough talking for now. We'd better get going again.' And off we went.

Hours passed.

Well, it was probably only twenty minutes, but it *felt* like hours. Turkeys are made to waddle free above the ground, not scrabble around in the dark underneath it.

Just when I thought I couldn't take it any more, Doc came to a halt. 'Right, Seamus. We're here.'

I was confused. 'Um, OK, Doc. But where is *here*, exactly?'

'Home.' He played the light of his torch over the tunnel wall, then reached out to a wooden strut that looked exactly like the thousands of other wooden struts we had passed

and pressed it. A portion of the wall next to us swung open, and I followed Doc through the opening into a cosy little room that I had definitely been in recently. He

shuffled across the room and twisted a little ornate knob on a chest of drawers, and the tunnel wall swung soundlessly shut behind us.

I had a look around the room, and it came to me – I was back in Doc's sitting room. I had called here less than forty-eight hours ago to get some dirt on Maurice Masher. I'd had a busy time since then. Maurice Masher and Simon the Snake had both been killed, and I was Suspect Number One for both murders.

Suddenly I felt very tired.

'I don't know what to do, Doc. I'm wanted for two murders and now I'm on the run from the police.'

'Don't worry, Seamus.' Doc was gently reassuring. 'I've been involved in this kind of case before. We'll figure out who did those murders and we'll ... find a way to square things with the cops. Elvis will be here tomorrow. They have to release her in the morning. So we'll make a plan then. Right now you need ... rest.'

'Y'know, Doc, this all started with Imelda Ermine and her damn €100 notes. Everything went downhill from when I met her.'

Doc gave a start. 'What do you know about ... Imelda Ermine?'

'Well, not a lot. She hired me to look into Simon, the owner of the Clubfooted Pigeon. She thought he was some kind of threat to Maurice Masher. And now I think she's trying to frame me for the murders.'

Doc looked worried. 'Maybe you're right. I've always been suspicious of … Miss Ermine. I didn't realise she was … mixed up in this. Anyway, we'll make a plan about it in … the morning.' He still looked worried as he showed me to the spare bedroom, but I was too tired to think any more about it.

'We'll make a plan in … the morning,' Doc said again as he closed the door.

The last thought I had before I drifted off to sleep was to remember where I had seen that locket before, the one that Elvis had swiped and that I had told her to put back. I had actually seen it twice. Each time it had been hanging on its expensive gold chain around Imelda Ermine's neck.

I don't remember thinking any more. I fell asleep and didn't dream.

16

DEAD ENDS

'Well, kiddo, how does it feel to be Public Enemy Number One? There's a huge manhunt under way for you. Or should I say a huge *turkey*hunt!' *Wink wink.* Elvis was in flying form, unfortunately.

We were in Doc's kitchen – Elvis, Doc and I – and we were having breakfast. It was the morning after my long crawl to freedom and we were trying to formulate a plan to prove my innocence. Unfortunately, we were getting nowhere fast. Even more unfortunately, Elvis insisted on seeing the funny side of everything. If she wasn't careful she'd be trying to seeing the funny side of being kicked out on her ear. That might be more of a challenge for her.

'I have to admit that Miss Ermine's … involvement in this is worrying.' Doc clearly hadn't known that Imelda Ermine was mixed up in all of this, and he was still coming to terms with it. 'And you're telling us, Seamus, that the gold locket … Elvis saw in the evidence tray, it was … hers?'

'Definitely, Doc. And what's more, the police found that locket at my office, tangled up in a mop. I hit the intruder with that mop before they ran off, which means that the intruder *must* have been Imelda Ermine.'

'But what would she have been doing there? Why break into … your office?'

'I was thinking about that, Doc. She must have been looking for my not-too-rusty shears. I mentioned them to her the day she came to see me. I'd say she broke in, took the shears and then used them to kill Simon. She left them at the scene of the crime to pin it on me. That's how she framed me for it.'

'Wowzers, kiddo! She sounds like one pretty cunning cat!' Elvis sounded very impressed, as one criminal busi-nesswoman to another. I wondered why she didn't just go ahead and nominate Imelda Ermine for the Craftiest Criminal of the Year Award.

'She has a history of … being cunning.' Moles always look worried. It just comes naturally to them. But Doc looked way, *way* more worried than was natural. Even for a mole. 'Remember I told you about those … Dalma-tians, Seamus? The ones who died when the … tunnels collapsed? Well, like I told you, Maurice … Masher inherited everything from two of them.' His look of concern deepened. 'Imelda Ermine inherited everything from … the third.'

'That seems pretty odd, Doc. How come?'

'He was her … husband.'

Wowzers was right. I nearly fell off my seat. This was big news. Although now that he said it, I remembered that Imelda Ermine had told me about her husband that first day we'd met.

'So you're telling me that Maurice Masher killed Imelda Ermine's husband? But that makes no sense! Why would she be so pally with Maurice now? Or, at least, before he died?'

Doc hummed. Then he hawed. Finally, he spoke. 'There were rumours at the time that … Imelda Ermine only wanted her husband for his … money. People said that she hatched a plot with … Maurice Masher to kill him and make it look like … an accident. Though nothing was ever proved. So maybe she was pally with … Maurice the whole time. Including when her husband was … killed.'

Elvis chimed in. 'And word on the street is that she stands to inherit the Blue Chameleon now that Maurice is out of the picture! Apparently Maurice left it to her in his will. That's two unfortunate deaths that Miss Ermine has done very well out of, kiddo. That cat is a real go-getter!' She just kept going up and up in Elvis's estimation. I wondered when Elvis was going to set up the Official Imelda Ermine Fan Club.

'Do we have any idea why she would have killed Simon? Is there any word on the street about that?'

'Not yet, kiddo. That one's a bit of a mystery. Certainly she's not in line to inherit the Clubfooted Pigeon. But she's a devilishly cunning cat, and I think we all agree that Simon's murder has her paw-prints all over it, so no doubt there's a good reason for it!'

'Well, my problem now is that, as far as I can see, this devilishly cunning cat has committed a double murder and gone and framed me for it!'

Doc, as ever, cut straight to the chase. 'Do we have any way of … proving any of this?'

'Well, Doc, there is the locket that Elvis took from the evidence tray. It doesn't prove that Imelda Ermine killed Simon and Maurice, but at least it shows that she broke into my office, so it's a start.'

Elvis coughed. 'I'm not sure it's that black-and-white, kiddo. After all, Miss Ermine could always say that she dropped it the day she came to hire you.'

'She could say that, but no-one would believe her. She never went into the broom closet, and the mop hasn't been out of the closet in months. At least not until I hit her with it. Auntie Et will back me up on that. And so will the state of the floor. So it's a good thing you put the locket back in the evidence tray, otherwise we'd have a hard time convincing the police that it's the same one they found in my office.'

Elvis gave another cough. And another one. Then she went bright red.

'Elvis, are you choking?' Doc made a start towards her, his face full of concern.

Elvis held up her hand, spluttering. 'Eh, no, no, Doc. I'm not choking. It's just that, well, I'm still not convinced that the locket would help us much. Even if I did put it back in the evidence tray.'

I suddenly developed a sneaking suspicion about Elvis and the locket and the putting-back-in-the-tray instruction. 'What do you mean *if* you did? Either you did or you didn't, Elvis. So, which is it? Did you put it back after I told you to?'

I've never seen such a sheepish look on a non-sheep. And certainly not on a meerkat.

'Well, kiddo, I actually didn't get a chance. The sniffers were all over me after you broke out. They didn't let me out of their sight until they released me.'

I was speechless. Elvis took advantage of my speechlessness to press on with the excuses. 'So, well, no. I didn't. But look on the bright side, kiddo, the very gold-coloured bright side! I know a flamingo who'll give us a great deal on a solid gold locket!'

I found my voice at last, and a very loud and voice it was. 'Elvis! How could you?'

'Did I say "us", kiddo? I meant you! He'll give *you* a great deal on it!'

'Deal? What deal? What are you talking about?'

'Freddie the Flamingo, kiddo! He won't ask any questions, he'll just hand over a wad of cash for it. Like you said, it's no good as evidence now. We'll never be able to persuade Dazzer and his sniffers that it's the same one that was in your apartment. And even if we could, it wouldn't look great that you stole it from Sniffer HQ.'

'But *I* didn't steal it, Elvis!' I wailed. '*You* did! After I told you not to!'

'Well, whoever actually stole it, it wouldn't look good if you walked back into Sniffer HQ waving it around. It would only give them something extra to arrest you for, on top of the double murder. Better off to go with Freddie, that's my advice.'

I was speechless again. Elvis could really have that kind of effect on you. Doc took the opportunity to pipe up.

'I think Elvis is … probably right, Seamus. At least about the locket … not being much help in … clearing your name right now. So the question is … what do we do?'

I didn't have an answer and, for once, neither did Elvis. So the three of us just sat there glumly, turning the problem over in our minds and coming up with nothing but dead ends that were every bit as dead as Simon the Snake and Maurice Masher.

17

THE CALL

A week later the three of us were in Doc's kitchen again, just as we had been most days since the break-out. It had been the longest week of my life, stuck in Doc's cramped subterranean digs with lots of stress and worry and precisely zero seconds of sunlight. I couldn't leave Doc's house, and twice I had to scramble off to hide in the tunnels when the police came to question Doc and search the place. Elvis was constantly popping in to share her latest hare-brained schemes to clear my name and the latest gossip doing the rounds about the Avian Assassin, aka Seamus the Shamus.

My week had been completely unpleasant, unproductive and underground. It turned out that being a fugitive from the law was absolutely no fun at all.

Then the phone rang.

Doc looked around, puzzled. 'I didn't know that the … phone still worked. I wonder who it … could be.'

'I don't know, Doc,' said Elvis, exasperated. 'But if you don't answer it we'll never find out!'

Doc shrugged, shuffled over and picked up the phone. Moles wouldn't be known for their keen sense of hearing, so the call automatically came out over a loud tinny loudspeaker.

'Hello. This is Doc.'

'I know dat. Dis is me.' The voice was loud, tinny and sounded like it would have difficulty with words of more than four letters. The loudness and tinnyness were probably the fault of the phone. The difficulty with words of more than four letters was probably the fault of the caller. A very piggy-sounding caller.

'Hello, me. Do you have a name that ... I could call you? If I call you "me", then this ... could get very confusing.'

There was a pause. Pigs' thoughts move pretty slowly, I suppose. Like glaciers. Or moss.

'You can call me Snoot.'

Well, that nailed it. It was my old friend Snot, the bouncer from the Clubfooted Pigeon. It had taken him half a minute to add an extra 'o' and come up with 'Snoot' as an alias. That sounded about right, given how difficult he had found it to follow a normal conversation when I had met him.

'OK, Mr Snoot. What can I do ... for you?'

'You know dat tur key.'

There was a pause. In the interests of keeping the conversation going, Doc eventually spoke up. 'I'm not sure if that's a statement or ... a question, Mr Snoot. I do know a turkey, but I ... don't know where he is.'

There was another pause. This was getting a bit tiring. I thought fleetingly about going to the kitchen to prepare an insect-based snack, but then decided to stick it out and try to hear all of the conversation over my grumbling stomach.

'You can gut a mess uge to de tur key?'

'Yes, I suppose I could get … a message to him. If it were important.'

You guessed it. Another pause. Then: 'You tell de tur key dat he need to meet me. I have inn fur may shun fur him. A bout dat cat. De one who sings.'

It was clear that the cat who sings was Imelda Ermine, but it took me a few seconds to put 'inn fur may shun' back together. I did it at just about the same time Doc did.

'What information do you have about … the singing cat, Mr Snoot?'

Yet another pause. Snot was thinking so hard I could nearly hear it over the tinny phone line. 'I tell dat to de tur key. I nut tell it to you.'

'OK, Mr Snoot. And when will you … tell it to him?'

This time the pause was shorter. Snot clearly had this bit prepared. 'He must come to de back room. Of de Club Foot Ed Pidge On. To mor oh. At mid night. He must come ah lone. And he must bring five hun dred your oh.'

Now the pause was on our end. Five hun dred your oh, or €500 as it was better known, was a lot of money. I had that much money, and more, at my office. Imelda

Ermine had been very generous with her payment. But my office was currently a crime scene so I couldn't really waltz back in there and pick it up. And I was fairly sure Doc wouldn't have that kind of money lying around. I didn't know about Elvis, but then, I didn't really know Elvis, so borrowing €500 from her might have been a stretch. I looked imploringly at Elvis and Doc. Doc looked at a loss, as he often did. Elvis, on the other hand, winked, reached into some secret inner pocket and drew out the locket. The very expensive gold locket, on the very expensive gold chain. I thought for a second and then nodded to Doc. As Elvis had said,

it wasn't going to help me clear my name with the police, so it might as well help me get me some info from a slightly crooked-sounding pig-bouncer.

'Well, Mr Snoot, the turkey can meet you … tomorrow. He doesn't have €500 but … he does have a very expensive gold … locket that he can give you. As payment.'

This was followed by the pause to end all pauses. If it weren't for the heavy breathing that was audible from time to time on the loudspeaker, I would have presumed that Snot had died. Or left the country. At long, long last: 'Dat will do. I will take de lock it. I will see de tur key to mor oh. Ah lone.'

And, with that, Snot hung up.

'I don't know, Seamus. I have a really … bad feeling about this.'

It was the following morning, and Doc was getting more and more worried about the meeting with Snot. Elvis, on the other hand, seemed all for it.

'Come on, Doc, live a little – it'll be good for the turkey to go on an adventure! And he might even clear his name. Anyway, you have a really bad feeling pretty much every time you get out of bed in the morning, but you still manage to do that!'

'I just don't trust that … pig at all. There's something fishy about … this set-up. It feels far too much like … a set-up.'

I wasn't about to tell Doc this, but I wouldn't trust that pig as far as I could throw him. And throwing huge muscle-bound pigs is definitely not something that turkeys are designed to do. But I was getting extremely itchy feet from being stuck in Doc's burrow for so long, so I was willing to grasp at any straw I was offered. Even a slightly suspicious piggy-smelling straw.

'There's nothing to it, Doc.' I wasn't nearly as confident as I sounded, but I put on a brave face and hoped that my bluffing would turn into real confidence before midnight, like a pumpkin turning into a fancy carriage. 'I'll waltz in, get the info, hand over the locket and waltz out again. Simple!'

Doc frowned. 'I really don't think … it will be that simple. Especially if you … go alone.'

'I don't know, Doc. In my experience, Snot is pretty simple. Even by pig standards. I can't imagine how it could be any more complicated than that.' Doc looked like he was going to speak again, but I ploughed on. 'Anyway, I'm the only one here who's Public Enemy Number One. It's my life on the line, so it's my call. I'm going, and I'm going alone. Full stop.'

Elvis gave me a conspiratorial smile and a wink. For once, I didn't even mind the winking.

The three of us set out at 11 PM. Doc brought us through the tunnels to a disused building just across the road from the Clubfooted Pigeon, so that I could avoid being outside for too long. The police were still looking for me, after all.

I was even more nervous than earlier – my pumpkin-nerves had yet to turn into the fancy carriage of confidence, and midnight was ticking closer and closer. Doc sounded even more breathless than usual from all the crawling, so he wasn't going to use up any of his precious breath on speaking. On the other hand, Elvis seemed to be thoroughly relishing the journey, occasionally singing snatches of pop songs under her breath. I suppose that enjoying this kind of thing so much was what got her put into jail twenty-six times. And being so good at it was what got her straight back out again each time.

We got to the spot just before midnight. It was eerily quiet inside the disused building. Which only made the occasional scratch and rustle even more frightening. I felt sick with nerves, but quitting just wasn't an option. As I like to say, turkeys aren't chickens. Especially when it comes to using pigs to catch killer cats.

Once Doc had caught his breath, he snorted. Then he harrumphed. Finally he spoke. 'Is there any chance you'll … change your mind? Or at least bring us … as back-up?'

'Thanks, Doc, but I have to do this alone. If Snot sees you, the deal is off and I might never clear my name. I don't think I can go through life living in those tunnels.

Turkeys were made to run free. Or at least waddle quickly free.'

Doc snorted again, but he seemed resigned to my decision.

Elvis held out her paw to me. 'You know, kiddo, if you do want to go in there alone, you could always bring this.'

It took a second before I realised what she was holding in her paw. It was small and gleamed darkly. Almost evilly. It was a gun.

'No way, Elvis! I've no idea how to use one of those. I'd be as likely to shoot my own foot as do anything useful with it!'

For the first time since I'd met her, Elvis seemed serious about something. Deadly serious. 'Snot mightn't be the brightest lightbulb in the box, Seamus, but he's a serious pig. And he could do serious damage to you if that's what he gets into his thick skull.' She paused. 'I hope you know how to take care of yourself in there.'

'So do I, Elvis. Because whatever else I do, I'm definitely not bringing that gun in with me. Anyway, if the police found me with a gun I'd be in serious trouble. Even *more* serious trouble.'

Elvis gave me a long look, then nodded. It was hard to figure out if she thought I was brave or mad or both.

Doc gave one last harrumph, but seemed to have given up on arguing. 'All right, Seamus, we'll wait … right here. Just in case. Give a shout if you … get into trouble. We'll be right there.'

'Thanks, Doc. And thanks, Elvis. I know you're only looking out for me. But I don't feel like I have a choice. This seems like my only shot at laying the Avian Assassin to rest.'

Somewhere far off, a bell began to toll the twelve long, slow knells of midnight.

It was showtime.

18

THE BACKROOM

The backroom of the Clubfooted Pigeon was quiet, plush and dark — a lot more luxurious than I had imagined it would be. Velvet curtains hung on all the walls. Expensive-looking lamps smeared a soft light over the room that just highlighted the shadows.

As my eyes adjusted to the understated lighting, I could make out a shape draped across one of the couches. A worryingly un-piggish shape. It shifted position slightly and I saw a row of pointed pearly teeth glisten in the gloom. Teeth that were well-brushed, well-flossed and very worryingly unpiggish.

I closed my eyes and gulped, hoping that when I opened them I'd realise I had been seeing things.

'Hi, Seamus.' I had forgotten her purr. My stomach did a quick series of backflips and I opened my eyes. Her teeth seemed to gleam even more pointedly than before. 'It's so *nice* to see you again.' She raised a paw and gave a little wave. Or maybe she was just showing off her perfectly manicured and razorsharp claws.

'Um, nice to see you too.' A pretty awful opening line I admit, but I wasn't at my most confident and relaxed. Suddenly I wished that I had brought Elvis and Doc with

me. Or at least Elvis's gun. I briefly thought about shouting for help, but I didn't think I'd even get the 'he–' out
before Imelda Ermine would have me silenced. For good.

'Really? You weren't expecting someone else?'

'Well, actually, now that you mention it, I was.'

Well, actually, now that you mention it, I was panicking. But I needed to play it cool. Obviously Imelda Ermine had done something to Snot, and whatever it was she had done to him, there was no doubt that she could do it to me a whole lot easier. All I could think was that the longer I kept her talking, the longer I stayed alive.

'Ah, yes,' she purred, 'the lovely Snot. He told me all about his phone call to Doc. It took a while. He doesn't use big words. Or long sentences. But he got there in the end. I was very interested in it, especially when I heard that you have my locket.'

God, she must have really done a job on Snot. By the sounds of it she had made him squeal like a, well, like a pig. Not easy to do with a pig as big and muscly as Snot. He didn't strike me as a pig who squeals.

'You must have a lot of questions about all of this, Seamus.'

I had so many questions I didn't even know where to start, but I had to play it cool in the hope of keeping her guessing. Better to let her think that I had it more or less figured out, even if I was completely in the dark, at sea and up the creek without a paddle.

'I do have one or two, Miss Ermine.'

'Well, have you opened my locket, Seamus?'

'Um, not yet, actually.' I couldn't believe that it hadn't occurred to me to open it before.

She smiled sweetly with her mouth, but her eyes remained cold. 'Why don't you start by doing that now? I presume you did bring it, that you aren't just bluffing.'

Slowly I took the locket out. It was surprisingly heavy. I turned it around with my feathers. It looked very old – maybe it was an antique? There was a tiny button on the side. I pressed it, and the locket sprang open.

Inside was a photograph of a dog. A Dalmatian.

Very softly, she said, 'That's my husband, Seamus. His name was Jeff. I loved him very much.'

'But I heard –'

Imelda Ermine hissed furiously at me and I stopped, taken aback. I had never seen her get really angry before. And now she was livid. 'You heard *what*? That I planned to kill him? That I organised that accident? Lies! I *loved* Jeff. And that horrible, *horrible* Maurice Masher killed him. *Murdered* him!'

'But Maurice Masher left you the Blue Chameleon in his will. Why would he do that if you hated him?'

Imelda Ermine smiled. It was the coldest smile I had ever seen. I remembered her smiling as she left my office, that first day I met her. That had been a frosty smile. This one was arctic. Someone who could smile like that was capable of anything. I shivered.

'Well, Seamus, Maurice didn't *know* that I hated him. I'm good at hiding things. Maurice fell in love with me when Jeff was still alive. That's why he made sure Jeff was in the tunnel when it collapsed. The other two mutts in there, he killed them to get their money. He faked their wills so that he'd inherit everything of theirs. That was just greed. But Jeff he killed to get me.

'I was furious, but I knew I couldn't prove anything. So I kept it all inside and pretended that everything was fine. People thought I had gotten tired of my husband, so I let them think that. I let *Maurice* think that. I let him believe that someday, maybe, I might love him back. Then one day he told me he had changed his will, that he was leaving everything to me. And I knew this was it.'

She stroked the arm of the sofa. I was hypnotised, afraid to move.

'That's where you came in. I made up a story about threats from the Clubfooted Pigeon. There never were any threats. But I needed to point the blame somewhere. So I framed Booger.'

I was confused. 'What? I thought you framed me!'

She smiled indulgently, as if she were explaining something very simple to a small child who just couldn't understand.

'After I killed Maurice, I started to frame Booger. I told you that I'd seen a pig around the time of the murder and left in just enough detail for you to identify him. But then I got to thinking, Seamus, that maybe I could also kill Simon and frame *you* for *both* murders! You'd mentioned those rusty shears of yours, and it occurred to me after I killed Maurice that they would be a very useful murder weapon. And a very *identifiable* murder weapon. If they were used to kill someone, you would definitely be the main suspect. So because of your shears, poor Simon came to a very messy end!'

'But why kill Simon? What did he have to do with your husband?'

'Nothing at all, Seamus! That one I did just for the money. With Simon gone, the Clubfooted Pigeon is in turmoil. And now I can come in like a fairy godmother and take it over, using all the money I'm inheriting from dear old Maurice!' She gave a low purr of satisfaction.

I was suddenly very angry. 'I can understand why you'd want Maurice dead. But killing Simon, that was just greed! That means you're no better than Maurice Masher!'

'Well, Seamus, what's the point in living if a cat can't buy fur coats and diamonds?'

She rose from the sofa and padded slowly across the room towards me. I backed away, afraid to let her get too near.

'Hang on a minute,' I said. 'When I was in the Blue Chameleon after Maurice had been killed I definitely smelled something fishy. Or, actually, I smelled something *piggy*. Booger *must* have been there that day!'

'I'm afraid not. Despite his bad taste in knuckle-piercings, Booger is entirely innocent in all of this. But you aren't completely wrong. There *was* a pig there that day. Snot wasn't visiting his granny, like he told the police. The police never checked out his granny story. If they had, they would have found out that his granny was busy that day, working as a bouncer at the Bruised Banana, and that she hasn't seen Snot in a month. Instead, Snot was visiting Maurice Masher. It was a very short, very sharp and very terminal visit.'

I felt my stomach drop away altogether. I had got it completely the wrong way around. Imelda Ermine hadn't made Snot tell her about the phone call to Doc. Snot had been working for her all along. Snot might have been every bit as simple as I thought he was, but Imelda Ermine wasn't. Not by a long way.

I thought that I had been about to cunningly collect evidence to clear my name and put Imelda Ermine behind bars. Instead, I had been walking right into her trap and presenting myself to her like a Christmas turkey: plucked, trussed and stuffed.

I was caught in the cat's claws and could see no way out.

19

ENDGAME

I gulped. 'So Snot works for you?' I asked miserably.

She laughed. A soft, tinkly laugh, with a deadly cruel heart.

'Of course he does! I snuck him into the club, and when he was finished with Maurice I snuck him out again. Snot used to work for Maurice years ago – they go way back – so I knew Maurice wouldn't raise the alarm when Snot dropped by for a friendly little visit. Then I told you I had seen a pig with pierced knuckles, and you identified Booger for me to the police. And poor old Booger would have been framed for the murder if I hadn't remembered those shears in your office and thought that I might be able to frame you instead, and get away with two murders. So I broke into your office and stole them.'

I was still trying to process Snot's new status.

'But why would Snot do it?'

'Why do most people do anything? For the money, what else? He earned next to nothing working as a bouncer. I promised to hire him as my personal bodyguard. Now he gets more money in a day than he used to earn in a month.'

She came towards me again, until we were nearly nose-to-beak. This time I was too overcome by it all to move, or to play for more time.

'Now, Seamus, my locket.' Her voice was low and hypnotic, nearly a whisper. 'You can give it back to me.' She reached out, extended one perfectly pointed claw and fished the locket from my unresisting feathers. 'Why, thank you, Seamus.' She raised her voice, as if talking to someone outside the room. 'And now, Snot, you might earn some of that huge salary of yours.'

It turned out she wasn't talking to someone outside the room. She was talking to someone behind one of the velvet curtains.

A curtain swished aside, revealing Snot. 'So, Mis Ter Tur Key. We meet again.'

Except this time, he was pointing a gun at me.

This night was getting worse by the minute. I had started to feel a little panicky earlier. Now I was at full-blown panic stations, with a side order of freaking out and extra panic sauce.

I could see Imelda Ermine next to me, her lips in a tight smile and the locket dangling from one of her paws. I could see Snot on the other side of the room, his gun pointed at my overlarge belly. I could see the lamps and the velvet curtains and the plush expensive carpet. I just couldn't move.

'You wunt me to shoot de tur key, Miss?' In fairness, Snot was nothing if not polite. I guess that's why she was paying him the big bucks. That, and his ability to 'take care of people'. And not in a Florence Nightingale sort of way.

'Not quite yet, Snot. I have other plans for him.'

Imelda Ermine looked delighted with herself, like the cat who had got the cream. If by 'the cream' you mean 'away scot free with two murders and stood to inherit an enormous amount of money', then I suppose she was.

She lowered her voice, leaned right in to me, and continued in a conspiratorial whisper. She was so quiet that at first I thought I must have misheard her. 'And the police definitely won't believe you once you've shot Snot.'

'What?!' I specifically hadn't brought a gun with me so nothing like this would happen. 'But I *won't* shoot Snot!'

'Dat's right, turkey. You not shoot Snot. *Snot* shoot *you.*' Snot seemed to be in agreement with me on the Seamus-won't-shoot-Snot front, although I didn't like his thinking on the Snot-will-shoot-Seamus front. But Imelda Ermine had other ideas. I could hear the tremor of excitement in her whisper.

'Well, Seamus, *I'll* know that you didn't shoot Snot. But sadly for you, the police won't. And when you shoot at me as well, I'll have no choice but to kill you. And I'll regret it terribly, but no-one will blame me for it. After all, it will just be self-defence. "Seamus the turkey," they'll say, "who knew that, under that mild-mannered exterior, he was really the Avian Assassin, one of those psycho turkeys who goes around killing people?" Goodbye, Seamus. It's been nice knowing you.'

Then, for the second time that week, a lot of things happened all at once.

There was the loud *crack* of a gun going off. I looked wildly around – the noise was so loud and the room was so small that it was hard to tell where it had come from.

Snot pitched forward and landed face-first on the floor. Dead.

Almost immediately there was a second *crack*, and Imelda Ermine gave a gasp.

I looked down and saw that her foot was bleeding. She had been shot.

I looked up again and saw her raise the gun towards me, her face disfigured by pain but still determined.

'Like I said, Seamus, it's been nice knowing you.'

The door burst open and Elvis charged in, waving a gun and shouting.

I fainted. It seemed like the most sensible thing to do.

I woke up when the alarm clock went off.

I sat straight up in bed, looked down and gave a startled gasp. I had hands, not wings. I wasn't a turkey!

It had all been a dream.

THE
END

AFTER THE END

OK, I'm just joking. Of course I don't have hands. Have you ever seen a turkey with hands? That would just be weird.

Still, I was pretty confused when I came to. What had just happened? And where was I? I remembered there had been soft lighting and velvet curtains. But now there were bright lights and beeping machines and I was lying in a bed with a wire hooked up to my wing.

I was in a hospital. I remembered now – I had fainted.

As if a dam had been released, all the memories came flooding back. The two gunshots. Snot falling forward, dead. Imelda Ermine bleeding. Then pointing the gun at me. And Elvis bursting in, yelling.

Uh oh. Imelda Ermine might not have been able to put the final part of her plan into action and finish me off, but I was pretty sure she was going to try to blame me for shooting Snot. And for the other two murders. And I wasn't sure how she had been shot in the foot, but I reckoned she was going to try to blame me for that too while she was at it. If she had managed to dispatch me as well, it would have been perfect. Apart from having a very sore foot. As it was, it was pretty damn good. Even taking the sore foot into account. Far too good for me to be relaxed about it.

I had to get to the police to explain what had really happened before she was able to spin them her story. I just hoped it wasn't too late.

I sat up in the bed and the machine next to me went berserk: flashing lights, alarm bells, the works.

Right on cue the door opened and Elvis and Doc came in.

'Good to see you awake, kiddo! Though you might want to lie back down. Those alarms will keep going bananas until you do!'

I lay back down in the bed. The alarms had made me realise that I had a terrible headache.

'How are you feeling … Seamus? You've been through … a lot.'

'I feel pretty awful, Doc, but I don't have time to worry about that now. I have to get to the police to explain what's going on before Imelda Ermine frames me. Again! She got Snot to kill Maurice Masher and she killed Simon with my not-too-rusty shears and she framed me for both of them. And then she shot Snot, right in front of me, and she's going to try to frame me for that too!'

Elvis and Doc grinned. Recently, when people had smiled it had spelt trouble for me. Thankfully, this time it didn't.

'Impressive detective work, kiddo. Although next time maybe you should listen to me so that you don't go and nearly get yourself killed before you figure it out!'

'So you knew it was Snot all along?!'

'We just found out, Seamus. Not long after … you did.'

'OK, Doc, so we need to go tell the police right now! There's not much point in *us* knowing. After all, I'm a wanted criminal, and you're not much better, Elvis. The only reason you're not locked up is that you keep breaking out. I can't see them believing something just because you tell them.'

'Lucky for you I don't have to tell them, kiddo! Snot did the telling. I just nodded along and kept pointing out that the sniffers had been after the wrong bird all along.'

This was very confusing. 'How could Snot do the telling? He was killed — I saw it!'

'You saw Snot fall over, Seamus. But he … wasn't killed. He just fainted, like you. Snot doesn't mind seeing … other people's blood. But he can't stand seeing … his own.'

'And that cat isn't as good a shot as she thought she was, kiddo!' This seemed to take Imelda Ermine down a few notches in Elvis's estimation. 'As far as Detective Dazzer can make out, she tried to shoot Snot. He was the last loose end, and she wanted to get rid of him to make sure she couldn't be tied to the first two murders. And to pin a third murder on you. But it was third time unlucky for Imelda! She only shot Snot in the leg. When he saw the blood, he passed out. And when he came round, Detective Dazzer had a chat with him and explained what he suspected him of doing. Then he explained it again in easy-to-understand words, and Snot admitted to it straight away.'

'Wait a minute. Dazzer has already been talking to Snot? So I'm in the clear?'

'Absolutely, Seamus. When Elvis burst in she ... managed to subdue Miss ... Ermine.' Elvis gave a big grin, clearly chuffed. 'We called Detective Dazzer ... straight away. He was very interested in the ... developments in the case.'

There was a knock on the door and, with perfect timing, in came Detective Dazzer. 'Seamus, I'm glad to see you're awake. You had a nasty fall back there. And nearly came to a much nastier ending. But at least things seem to have been straightened out.'

Elvis pulled a face behind Dazzer's back, but I was just relieved. 'So I'm really in the clear?'

'You certainly are. I never really thought that you did it, but after we found the shears we had to go through the motions of bringing you in. I was afraid that, if we didn't, Miss Ermine would have figured something was up and might have made a run for it.'

'So you knew it was her the whole time?'

'Well, I wouldn't say I knew it was her, but she was always number one on our list. I tried to warn you about her when we met in the Blue Chameleon, but I didn't think you were too receptive to my advice. So I sent Cheddar and Stilton around to check on you later that evening and make sure you weren't getting yourself into even more trouble. Lucky for you I did, or you might have been another of Miss Ermine's victims.'

That was a sobering thought – I had nearly forgotten that last night wasn't the first time I had fallen foul of Imelda Ermine.

'I had most of the pieces figured out before last night. Snot helped me put the final few in place. He filled me in on why she had Maurice and Simon killed. One for love and one for money, it would appear.'

'She told me all about it just before she tried to kill me.' There was silence in the room. I think we all realised just how close I had come to an early ending. 'Where is she now, Detective? She was shot as well, though I'm not sure how.'

'She's in a cell in the station. I think she shot herself in the foot. She was going to say that you did it, and was about to shoot you when Elvis arrived on the scene. As far as I can make out, she would have said that she had shot you in self-defence. We would have had a hard time proving that she hadn't.'

Suddenly all Imelda Ermine's talk about me shoot-ing her, and her shooting me in self-defence, made a lot more sense. Elvis had been right. She was some cat.

Somehow, that just made me feel sadder about the whole messy business.

Dazzer continued. 'There'll be a trial, and hopefully she'll go to jail for a very long time. Snot will testify, and the locket helps, as corroboration. If she told you everything, we'll need to take a statement from you about it. And we might need you to testify.'

I nodded glumly. It wouldn't give me any pleasure, but I would do what was needed. 'She loved her husband, you know.' After all she'd done, I didn't know why I felt like I should stick up for Imelda Ermine. But I did. A little bit, anyway. 'She really did. I think something in her changed when he died.'

There was a pause. I couldn't believe that it was over. Dazzer nodded. 'I think you're probably right, Seamus. But she still did what she did. Anyway, you need some rest. Take it easy. I'll be seeing you around, I'm sure.'

I never saw Imelda Ermine again. She confessed – eventually – so I didn't need to testify.

I spent two days in the hospital recovering. Doc and Elvis spent most of that time with me. On day two I got around to asking Elvis how she had managed to get into the backroom of the Clubfooted Pigeon so quickly if she'd been hiding across the street when the gunshots went off. She winked and told me she'd reckoned the gun should be in the room to defend me, whether I was the one holding it or not. Seeing as I wasn't willing to do the holding, she was more than happy to do it for me.

A few minutes after I left for the meet, she had sneaked across the road and into the club. She was trying to figure out which room I was in when the gunfire started. In principle I wasn't too happy that she had come after me, but in practice I was very relieved. Turns out she didn't just have a knack for getting herself out of sticky situations at just the right time.

Once I was discharged from the hospital and got back to the office, I found that Dazzer had got my broken window fixed. It was his way of saying thanks, I suppose.

I told Auntie Et to take two weeks off, paid leave. I still had no idea what I was paying her, but I didn't care. After the money from Imelda Ermine, I could certainly afford it. And to clear my head I knew I needed peace and quiet, rather than a bad-tempered hyena and quiet.

I set about getting rid of anything that might remind me of the case, and of Imelda Ermine in particular. I'd had enough of her to last me a lifetime. I threw out the cup she'd drunk from. I gave the chair she sat in to charity. I tidied up the mess she'd made when she broke in. I didn't get rid of absolutely everything, of course – I'm not crazy. I kept the money. To paraphrase a cat I once knew, what's the point in living if a turkey can't buy deep-fried grub balls and a new bed?

I still wasn't feeling quite myself about ten days later, when the doorbell rang.

'It's open!' I shouted from where I was sprawled on the far-too-small office couch. I hadn't taken on any work since the case had finished, and I didn't really feel like starting now. But there was no further noise from outside the door, so I hauled myself up and grumblingly headed out to see who was there. Maybe it wasn't someone looking to hire me – maybe someone was sending me flowers. Though on second thoughts, probably not.

A big cardboard box was sitting in the corridor right outside my door. There was no sign of anyone around. Clearly, whoever had delivered it had legged it straight away.

I took a closer look at the box. There was no address on it, just a handwritten note that read: 'To Seamus the Shamus. I thought you might want these back. Kind regards, Detective D.'

I opened the box. Inside were my not-too-rusty shears.

With a smile I picked them up. I turned them over, examining them carefully. They were mine all right – there was no way I could mistake them. They nearly got me sent to jail for life for a double murder I didn't commit. Them, and Miss Imelda Ermine.

I walked back into the office and dumped them in the bin.

Now I was ready for my next case.

THE
END

(FOR REAL, THIS TIME)

ABOUT THE AUTHOR

Jed Lynch is a human author from Ireland. He has co-written a number of plays, including one about a floating house and another about a giant singing brain. *Murder Most Fowl* is the first thing that he has co-written with a turkey. Seamus, a private detective who just happens to be a turkey, provides the exciting storylines based on the cases he has worked, as well as all of the feathers, wings and beaks in the partnership. Jed, on the other hand, provides the hands. He has a pet reindeer and is learning to play the trumpet.

ABOUT THE ILLUSTRATOR

Stephen Stone comes from the north-east of England where they are known as Sand Dancers. He's illustrated many picturebooks worldwide and loves to illustrate animals. Seamus is his first turkey detective and has now been added to his top ten list of favourite things to draw. He gets help with his creations from his studio assistant, a slightly aloof orange cat called Vincent Van Mog, who helps him choose all his colours.

ABOUT LITTLE ISLAND

Little Island Books is Ireland's only English-language publisher that publishes exclusively for young readers. Based in Dublin, it has been publishing books for children and teenagers since 2010. Little Island specialises in new Irish writers and illustrators, and also has a commitment to publishing books in translation. In 2019 Little Island was the Irish winner of *The Bookseller* magazine's first ever Small Press of the Year award.

www.littleisland.ie